My So-Called Phantom Love Life

Tamsyn Murray was born in Cornwall in the Chinese Year of the Rat. This makes her charming, creative and curious (on a good day) but also selfish, restless and impatient (v. v. bad day).

After moving around a lot during her early years, she now lives in London with her husband and her daughter. At least her body does. Her mind tends to prefer imaginary places and wanders off whenever it can but that's not necessarily a bad thing in a writer.

When she isn't making things up, you might find Tamsyn on the stage, pretending to be someone else. She occasionally auditions for TV talent shows. One day she might get past the first round . . .

Find out more about Tamsyn at her website:
www.tamsynmurray.co.uk

Also by Tamsyn Murray:

My So-Called Afterlife
My So-Called Haunting

My So-Called Phantom Love Life

TAMSYN MURRAY

PICCADILLY PRESS • LONDON

First published in Great Britain in 2011
by Piccadilly Press Ltd,
5 Castle Road, London NW1 8PR
www.piccadillypress.co.uk

A catalogue record for this book is available
from the British Library

ISBN: 978 1 84812 134 8 (paperback)

1 3 5 7 9 10 8 6 4 2

Printed in the UK by CPI Bookmarque, Croydon, CR0 4TD
Cover design by Patrick Knowles

To my parents, for teaching me to read.

Chapter 1

I knew the boy was different when I saw him walk on water.

Me and my mates were on the Serpentine in Hyde Park, messing about in a rowing boat. The April sun was burning off the afternoon clouds and Megan was daring Charlie to splash a group of French boys with the oars.

'Go on, Charlie,' she urged, stretching out a foot to kick him lightly on the shin. 'My family is descended from French aristocrats murdered in the revolution. They demand that I avenge their deaths.'

I grinned. That was a good one; Megan was about as French as a Cornish pasty and if the ghosts of her ancestors were demanding anything, it wasn't that she flicked algae-filled lake water over some innocent teenage tourists. In fact, as I gazed around the lake, I could see there was only one ghost nearby and he didn't look like he was auditioning for *The Scarlet Pimpernel.* He was wearing a killer pair of ripped jeans for a start. And did I mention he was walking on the water?

Megan was still nagging at Charlie. 'Where's your sense of patriotism? Stand up for your country!'

Charlie pushed his fringe carefully out of his eyes. 'How is starting a water fight in any way patriotic? The pond police will just kick us off the lake.'

I let their bickering fade into the background as I studied the ghost. He was now hovering near the island in the centre, watching the boats circling around him with an expression of amusement on his face. It was hard to be sure but I guessed he was a couple of years older than me – sixteen or seventeen. He looked relaxed and I wondered if he'd died in the park or whether he was drawn by the people who were enjoying the spring weather.

'No one is flicking anything at anyone. If you two have finished squabbling, do you think we could go that way?' I said, pointing over at the island as curiosity got the better of me.

Charlie dipped the oars into the water and we moved slowly away from the French boys.

'I might have known you'd side with them,' Megan grumbled, jerking her head towards the receding boat. 'Didn't Miss Pointer say Scotland and France were practically married in history last week?'

I pulled a face. I'd lived in Edinburgh most of my life, until my move to London six months before to live with my aunt, but I didn't have strong feelings one way or the other towards the French. Their language was another thing entirely, though; I'd give up Krispy Kreme for a month to drop those lessons. '*Où est la gare?*' with a soft Scottish burr was pretty much incomprehensible.

'I'm not siding with anyone. I'd just rather you didn't recreate the Battle of Trafalgar in the middle of Hyde Park. And since there are five of them and only three of us, we'd probably lose.'

Megan shook out her chestnut hair and let her fingers trail in the water. 'What's so interesting about the island, anyway? You know we can't go on it.'

She was right; there was a spiky chain linking the frequent metal posts, presumably so no one landed and disturbed what looked like birds' nests in the wooded undergrowth. It didn't matter. All I wanted was to get near enough to the ghost to figure out if he needed my help but I could hardly tell Megan that. She had no idea I was psychic and I had no intention of letting her find out. Instead, I pretended to peer at the trees and watched Mr Ripped Jeans. Now that we were closer, I could see that his brown hair gently curled against his head and that he was quite good-looking, in a Disney-Channel way. Charlie pulled at the oars again and we drew closer. I squinted in the sunshine, barely able to make out the distinctive blue glow the dead had; forget quite good-looking, this ghost was gorgeous. And the puckered scar which ran from one ear down to the corner of his mouth gave him an attractive roguish air.

'Hello? Wake up, Skye.' Megan waved a hand in front of my face. 'Do we have to go this way? Only there's a swan coming and it doesn't look too friendly.'

I followed her nervously pointing finger. Rounding the island behind the ghost was a large swan. Its beak was open and I could hear a low hissing noise. It definitely did not look happy.

The ghost heard it too and turned, just as the swan passed through him. Briefly, I wondered if he was the reason it was looking so menacing but Megan's agitation drove the thought from my head. She pulled at Charlie's sleeve. 'Row the other way!'

'Get off, Megan!' Charlie said, grappling with the oar as she tugged at his arm. It slid out of his grasp and the boat rocked as Megan wriggled around in her seat.

The ghost was watching the swan approach us now, frowning.

'Calm down, Megan,' I said, clutching the edge of my seat. 'It'll just go around us.'

Her eyes were wide with fear. 'No, it won't. I've heard about this. Swans can break your arm if you get in their way.'

I was pretty sure that was a myth but the swan was

opening its great white wings and suddenly the idea that it could hurt us didn't seem so unlikely. I could see why she was scared.

'Megan, sit down —' I began but it was too late; Megan was on her feet. The boat lurched crazily. Her arms flailed as she struggled to stay upright. Charlie lost his grip on the second oar and it splashed into the water.

'Nice one, Megan,' Charlie said, scrambling towards the side of the boat and thrusting an arm deep into the water. 'Are you trying to tip us over?'

Megan's eyes were still fixed on the swan, which was rearing up, its wings scything through the air. Its beak was wide as it bore down on us. A look of terror on her face, Megan craned backwards. The boat dipped with her weight. She screamed as we tilted towards the surface of the water and then we were over.

The lake was glacial, in spite of the warm day. Shock coursed through me as the chill savaged my nerve endings and, for several long seconds, I plunged into the murky depths without doing anything to stop my descent. Then survival instinct took over and my legs lashed out to propel me upwards. I gasped as I broke the surface and gulped in a lungful of air before looking round for my friends.

Charlie was about a metre away, clinging to the boat and coughing. The swan fired baleful glares our way as it glided back towards the island. There was no sign of Megan.

'Where is she?' I called, casting around to find her.

'D-Don't kn-know,' Charlie sputtered in between coughs. 'Under the boat?'

Other boaters were heading our way. Some were laughing but a few mirrored my concern. I twisted around in the water, desperate to see Megan's head break the surface. When seconds ticked past and there was no sign of her, I started to panic. Hadn't she said she could swim when the boat attendant had offered us life jackets? I bit my lip as I trod water. Now that I thought about it, there'd been a faint look of revulsion on her face when she'd eyed the orange plastic; what if she'd lied? I'd only known her for six months but Charlie had known her longer. Why hadn't he said anything?

Plunging back into the brown depths, I peered around. The lake wasn't that deep, she couldn't have gone far. Even so, fear flowed through me and my blood pounded in my ears. It had only been a minute since the boat tipped over; how long did it take to drown?

Charlie's legs swam into view as I cut through the water. Dark shapes loomed overhead – they'd be the other boats, I guessed. I couldn't see Megan anywhere. My lungs started to burn. Feeling the sting of tears, I kicked upwards.

Above the water, Charlie had got his breath back and was now looking as panic-filled as I felt. He was ignoring offers to climb into one of the boats and was shouting Megan's name as he scanned the lake. I could see one of the lake attendants heading our way in a motorboat but his progress was hampered by the other people on the lake. If Megan was drowning, he wouldn't reach us in time.

Then I saw the ghost. He was peering down at a patch of water about fifteen metres away, thrusting an arm into the water and drawing it out over and over. His expression was a tense mix of sorrow and anxiety, as though he wanted to pull something out but couldn't. Instantly, I realised why; Megan was there.

Swimming faster than I ever had before, I ploughed towards him. As I got closer, I could hear his feverish muttering. 'Take my hand, just take it. Please . . .'

Our eyes met for a second and surprise flickered in his. But I had no time to explain. Sucking in a deep breath, I forced myself back under the surface. Once again, my vision adjusted to the greenish-brown half-light and I caught sight of something dark red floating below me. I kicked down hard. It was the end of Megan's silk scarf. Spreading my fingers, I waved an arm beneath it and almost sobbed when they entangled in a web of fine strands; her hair. I closed my fingers and tugged. The strands became taut as her weight pulled against them. She must have felt the drag because she struggled and one of her flailing arms caught my ankle. I could have sobbed with relief – she was still alive. Forcing myself further down, I groped around for her face and slid my hands under her chin, pulling her towards me. Her eyes latched onto mine, wide and desperate, hands clutching at me as she writhed. Her added weight only dragged me down and we sank further towards the bottom of the lake.

My lungs were on fire and every cell was screaming for oxygen but there was no way I was leaving her. Summoning one last burst of energy, I wrapped my arms around her and thrust downwards once more. Mercifully, my feet thudded into the lakebed and the impact sent us catapulting through the water. The momentum only carried us so far, though. My feet flapped furiously as I strived to reach the precious air above us. It was so tantalisingly close but I couldn't seem to get there. Feeling as though my heart was about to burst, I kicked frantically. It was no use. Megan was wriggling in my arms and I struggled to keep hold of her. The last of my strength faded and we started to sink.

Something latched onto the back of my shirt. I shot upwards, my fingers clutching onto Megan. Then my hands lost their grip and she was dragged away from me. I opened my mouth to scream at the exact second my head broke the surface. Water rushed in and filled my lungs. I coughed as a pair of strong arms hauled me into a boat. Eyes streaming, I shook off the blanket someone was trying to wrap around me and scrambled to a sitting position.

'Megan —' I croaked, leaning over the edge to stare into the water.

'She's safe, don't worry,' a voice soothed and I looked up into the eyes of the lake attendant.

I refused to believe him. 'Where is she?'

He pointed to another boat a short distance away. 'She's there, bringing up what looks like half the lake.'

I peered across the water. Relief flooded through me as I saw Megan's soaking chestnut head retching exactly where he'd said she was. 'And Charlie?'

'He's on dry land, being checked over by paramedics. Which is where you're going now,' he said, and a hint of a smile hovered around his mouth. 'The Serpentine is clean but it's not meant for drinking. Next time you're thirsty, stick to Evian.'

It was the worst joke I'd ever heard but I didn't have the energy to tell him so. He nodded at the other man in the boat, who I hadn't even noticed was there. The engine gunned and we started towards the shore. Huddled on the floor, the last of my adrenaline drained away and I began to shiver as the realisation of what could have happened sunk in. How close had we come to drowning? And what would have happened if the ghost hadn't shown me where Megan was? My shuddering intensified as my thoughts darkened. Teeth rattling against one another uncontrollably, I forced myself to scan the lake for the ghost but I couldn't focus well enough to see very far and everything seemed blurred. I'd find him later and say thanks, I told myself, forcing my twitching fingers to hold onto the blanket. It was the least I could do, after all. Without him, my best friend might be a ghost too.

Chapter 2

When I was a kid I'd dreamed about travelling in an ambulance with the blue lights flashing and the siren blaring, but I'd always been the driver rather than the patient. So I wasn't fully able to appreciate the journey from Hyde Park to the A&E at University College Hospital. I was worried sick about Megan and it felt like I'd swallowed most of the Serpentine. It roiled around in my stomach as we sped around the corners, making me wonder if I was actually going to throw up all over Charlie.

The paramedic looked up from measuring my blood pressure. 'Keep the mask over your mouth,' she instructed in a kind voice. 'You need that oxygen.'

I lay back on the metal trolley bed and did as I was told, trying to stop trembling. There must have been two or three blankets on top of me, as well as the one around my shoulders but I still felt cold. Charlie was hunched on a fold-down seat opposite me, wrapped in a blanket, his eyes fixed anxiously on me.

'You OK?'

I nodded and lifted the oxygen mask a little. 'Yeah, except this thing smells worse than your PE socks.'

A reluctant smile tugged at the corners of Charlie's mouth. 'Nothing smells worse than my PE socks.' He thought for a moment. 'Except maybe yours.'

'Ha ha.' I considered reaching out a soggy leg to kick him but it felt as though it was made of granite. The paramedic was watching anyway, and I didn't think she'd approve of me inflicting actual bodily harm on another patient.

Charlie's smile evaporated. 'How do you think Megan is?'

I didn't have the first clue. She'd been alive when they'd bundled her into the other ambulance and sped away but that was all I knew. How long had she been underwater, struggling to break the surface? Had she lost consciousness?

'I don't know,' I admitted. 'Maybe they'll let us see her when we get to the hospital.'

The paramedic shook her head. 'Not for a while. She'll go straight to the ICU and you two will need tests to make sure you haven't done any lasting damage.'

She must have seen the panic on our faces because her expression softened and she patted my arm. 'Try not to worry. I'm sure she'll make a full recovery.'

Charlie's head drooped and his gaze became fixed on the floor. I placed the mask back over my mouth and stared up at the white ceiling. In my mind, the crimson tassels of Megan's scarf floated and danced, as though taunting me for not finding her sooner. Her pale face flashed before me and I recalled her terrified look as we sank further into the murky depths. The way my lungs had seared in pain as they screamed out for air would stay with me forever. My heart sped up, making the monitor beside me beep in shrill warning. The paramedic raised her head and stared at me sharply. Closing my eyes, I forced the memories away and the beeps started to slow. I wiped my suddenly sweaty palms on the blanket and breathed in and out as slowly as I could, reminding myself we'd survived. Thank God the lake attendants pulled us out when they did. The alternative would be giving me nightmares for weeks.

'So it really was a very lucky escape; all three of them have avoided permanent damage.' The doctor, whose name-badge proclaimed that he was Dr Mohammed, rubbed his face and offered my aunt, Celestine, a tired smile. 'Megan will need to stay in for observation but Skye is well enough to go home.'

It was three hours after my journey in the ambulance. Celestine and her boyfriend, Jeremy, had arrived almost immediately and kept me company through a barrage of tests and questions to check for brain damage or memory loss; if one more person asked me who the Queen of England was I'd scream. Now both of them were stood at the side of my bed and Celestine's gaze was focused a little above the man's head. I wondered if she was studying his aura to see if he was telling the truth about Megan but then she nodded. 'Thank you. I'm sure Skye will be glad to hear that.'

She had that right. Hospitals were grim enough at the best of times but they were a thousand times worse for psychics like me and her. Just think about the number of people who are wheeled in through the front doors and never wheeled out again alive – hospitals are Ghost Central. I'd already seen more than my fair share of ghostly bum cheeks peeking through hospital gowns that didn't quite cover everything at the back and it was only a matter of time before one of the ghosts clocked that I could see them. It might be selfish but I really couldn't handle a conversation with one of them and I'm sure my aunt felt the same. Jeremy should be grateful he's only part psychic.

'Can I see Megan before I go?' I asked.

Dr Mohammed shook his head. 'She's resting at the moment. Why don't you come back tomorrow, once you've had some sleep yourself?'

He was probably right; I did need to recover. My legs felt like I'd just finished a cross-country race and my chest ached when I breathed. They'd let Charlie go about an hour before. I'd seen his mum wrap him in an enormous hug and she'd squeezed her eyes shut as though trying not to cry. Charlie had endured the cuddle for thirty seconds before shaking her off, muttering, but secretly I think he'd enjoyed it.

'Thank you, Doctor,' Celestine said, putting her arm around me. 'We'll make sure she gets plenty of rest.'

Smiling, Dr Mohammed said, 'And save your swimming for the pool in future. The Serpentine is no place to practise your backstroke.'

He chuckled and I forced a grin onto my face. First the lake attendant and now the doctor; was everyone a comedian these days?

'Trust me,' Jeremy said, ruffling my matted blond hair in a way that I'd told him a zillion times I hated. 'Skye is going to be steering clear of lakes for some time.'

'Listen to your parents, young lady,' Dr Mohammed admonished, pulling the curtains around my bed. 'And stay out of trouble.'

He nodded to Jeremy and Celestine, who both looked as though they couldn't decide if they were insulted or amused at being mistaken for my mum and dad, and left. I swallowed my laughter and decided Dr Mohammed needed to go to Specsavers; OK, so Jeremy was dressed as though he'd been on a shopping spree in Age Concern but Celestine looked more like my older sister than my mother. Both of them had blond hair but since neither was over thirty, they'd have needed to start pretty young to have a fourteen-year-old daughter.

The comment got me thinking about my own mum and whether or not I should tell her about my brush with the lake-monsters. She was a few months into a year-long placement studying sea-horses on the Great Barrier Reef in Australia and, as far as I could tell, she was having the time of her life. She missed me, of course, but we spoke on Skype a couple of times a week, which was why I'd have to decide whether she needed to know the details of my adventure. I could always tell her I was looking for evidence of freshwater sea-horses – then again, maybe that wasn't the best idea I'd ever had.

'I think we'll play down the drama when we speak to your mum about this.'

I jumped as Celestine's voice cut into my thoughts. How did she know what I was thinking? She'd always promised me she couldn't read minds but I had my doubts. One thing I did know; if she'd been alive in any century other than the twenty-first, she'd have been charged with witchcraft.

'Fine by me,' I replied, trying not to look unnerved. 'She'd probably feel like she should come home.'

It wasn't strictly true. I loved my mum; after my dad's death, she'd brought me up alone but she didn't have her family's psychic gift like me. Once she'd realised her young daughter did, her attitude had subtly changed. It was as though she tucked part of herself away from me and I couldn't reach her the way I had when I was very small. I'd changed, too, and inevitably grown closer to Celestine over the psychic ability we shared, all of which meant that my mum was a little slow to come running when I needed her. I didn't blame her; it was just how it was.

Celestine handed me a small rucksack full of clothes, sympathy etched on her face. 'Well, no harm done. Let's not worry her.'

While Celestine and Jeremy waited outside my cubicle, I pulled on the clothes they'd brought and tried not to mind that the Oscar the Grouch T-shirt was one I normally wore in bed. Tugging the hairbrush through my tangled locks, I wondered how the two of them would react when I told them about the ghost at the lake. I'd seen the fear in Celestine's eyes when they'd first arrived at the hospital, followed by relief when she realised I was OK. I didn't think either of them would be keen for me to go back to the Serpentine again, even if there was a good reason. If I wanted to thank the boy at the lake, I'd have to do it on the quiet.

Chapter 3

I slept for fourteen hours and didn't dream once. When my grumbling stomach finally forced me downstairs in search of food, I found that Celestine had gone to work at the Church of the Dearly Departed – a spiritualist church – and Jeremy was reading the Sunday papers at the kitchen table.

'Afternoon,' he said, lowering the sports pages. 'How are you feeling today?'

'Hungry,' I said and slotted some bread into the toaster. 'But otherwise OK.'

He nodded. 'Good. Your aunt rang the hospital. Megan is up to having visitors if you want to go.'

I thought for a minute. If I wanted to take a detour to Hyde Park, I'd need to work out the timing carefully. With luck, I could get in and out of the hospital without bumping into any ghosts and then head to the Serpentine to see the one I did want to see. 'When are visiting hours?'

His gaze flicked to a piece of paper on the table. 'Between two and four, then from six till eight. I can drive you if you like?'

Normally, I'd jump at the offer of a lift but it didn't fit in with my plans. Shaking my head, I said, 'I'll get the bus and walk. After that mammoth sleep I could do with some fresh air.'

If he thought my sudden desire to use public transport was odd, he didn't mention it and I thanked my lucky stars Celestine was at work; she was much harder to fool. Grabbing my toast, I reached for the butter.

'How did West Ham get on yesterday?' I asked, nodding at the paper. I'd never really been into football until I'd met Dontay, the ghost of a talented young player who'd died in a gang-related shoot-out the previous year. He'd turned up at the Dearly D, and before I knew it my aunt had roped me in to talk to him. Dontay had eventually moved on to the astral plane, where ghosts go after they leave the earthly realm, but some of his passion for football must have rubbed off because I was now a firm follower of the Hammers.

Jeremy peered at the paper. 'They won two-nil and are up to tenth place in the league. Dontay would approve.'

I smiled. Until recently, Jeremy had only ever seen one

ghost, a teenage girl called Lucy. He knew there were spirits everywhere, even though he couldn't see them, like the ghost of the sixteenth-century witch who haunted our house. Personally, I thought Jeremy was lucky he couldn't see Mary; with her rotten stumpy teeth, bird's-nest grey hair and ragged clothes, she looked like a walking advert for the Black Death, but underneath her crusty exterior lurked a kind heart. And, thanks to Dontay's influence, she was now a West Ham fan too.

Jeremy glanced at the clock. 'Hadn't you better get ready?'

Yikes, he was right; although I'd showered as soon as I got home the night before, I could still smell pond slime in my hair and wanted to wash it again. I hadn't exactly been at my best the last time I'd seen the boy at the lake. The least I could do was look half-decent when I thanked him for saving my best friend's life.

Megan was ecstatic when I turned up at the hospital. Once she'd reassured herself I was OK, she admitted that her mum had forgotten to bring any make-up. I reckoned I knew the real reason she was pleased to see me, then: she was worried Charlie would see her *au naturel*. Although she'd known him since nursery school, it wasn't until Year Eight that Megan had developed a crush the size of Scotland on Charlie. They'd become friends through the school athletics teams, but she refused to tell him how she felt and instead lived in desperate hope that he'd somehow work it all out so that they could live happily ever after. It hadn't happened yet. She made me leave my make-up bag with her when my visit was over and had waved from behind my compact mirror as I'd left. I wondered if her brush with death would make her brave enough to tell him how she felt. The idea made me smile. Poor Charlie wouldn't know what had hit him.

Hyde Park was busy when I got there, full of families and couples enjoying the mild weather. I didn't have any trouble spotting the ghost, though; he was the one hovering on the water. It made getting close to him tricky; he was in the middle of the lake and there was no way I was getting in another boat. I settled on a deserted bench overlooking the island and waited for him to notice me watching him. It didn't take long.

His gaze flickered over me several times before coming to rest on my face. I guessed he must be questioning whether I really was staring at him. He drifted closer. I kept my eyes fixed on him. When he was almost at the edge of the water, I fired a deliberate smile his way. Then I touched the hands-free mobile phone earpiece I wore when I thought I might need to talk to someone no one else could see.

'Hi.'

The ghost stopped. The sunlight wasn't as bright as it

had been the day before and the faint blue outline which surrounded him was clearer; if the whole walking on water thing hadn't given him away, the glow would have.

He threw an uncertain glance over his shoulder, and then peered at me again, as though he couldn't believe I might be talking to him.

'I've come to say thank you for yesterday,' I went on, raising my voice so it would carry. 'If you hadn't shown me where my friend was, we probably wouldn't have got to her in time.'

If I hadn't had his attention before, I definitely did now. 'You can see me?'

Smiling, I nodded. 'Yeah. I'm psychic. I see loads of ghosts.'

His eyebrows shot up. 'Really? I always thought all that talking to the dead stuff was fake. You know, things hustlers said when they were trying to fool people into giving them money.'

I didn't blame him; I'd heard some terrible stories about so-called psychics telling people that Auntie Florence was happy in heaven and then charging them a fortune. It was called 'cold reading', when the pretend psychic picked up unconscious clues from their victim's responses and used them to reveal things they couldn't possibly 'know'. Television programmes about paranormal investigations didn't help, either. *The Ghost's The Host*, a show on one of the satellite channels, was by far the worst offender and ticked all the hokum psychic boxes. I wouldn't have been surprised if Scooby Doo and his gang had appeared as celebrity guests.

'Psychics do get a bad press,' I conceded, 'but that doesn't mean we're all frauds. I don't suppose you believed in ghosts either.'

Head tilted to one side, he studied me for a moment, and then grinned ruefully. 'You've got a point. There are a lot of things I believe in now that I didn't before.'

When he smiled it transformed the right-hand side of his face from Disney Channel boy-next-door to model material. The smile didn't extend as far on the other side, making his expression wryly lopsided and I guessed that whatever had given him the scar had caused some nerve damage as well. I wanted to ask where he'd got it. Ghosts appeared exactly as they had the moment they'd died, but this wasn't an injury from his death – the skin had knitted together to leave a silvery puckered trail across his otherwise smooth cheek, suggesting an old wound. It must have been the stuff of horror stories when it had happened and I couldn't help wondering how he'd coped with such a terrible disfigurement. Did that have anything to do with his death?

With a jolt, I realised I was staring and a burning wave of embarrassment washed over me. Before I could apologise, the ghost spoke again. 'Before I died, I got used to my scar being the first thing people noticed but lately I've forgotten what it's like.' His tone was light as he touched his cheek. 'I suppose you want to know how it happened.'

A woman with a dog was heading our way. At first, I thought the terrier would refuse to pass us. He growled at the boy and bared his teeth but the tail between his legs told me it was fear rather than aggression. I stayed silent as his owner tried a mixture of persuasion and irritation to drag him past my bench, distracted by the ghost's words. I was curious about his scar but I wouldn't have dreamed of mentioning it. Then again, he'd raised the subject, which could mean he wanted to talk. As soon as the woman had pulled the dog away and they were out of earshot, I fixed my gaze back on the ghost. 'Not if you don't want to tell me.'

He spread his hands. 'As long as you don't mind talking here. For some reason I can't leave the lake. It's like there's an invisible forcefield in the way.'

'You're tied to the place where you died,' I explained. 'Every ghost is. It's called your haunting zone and the only way you can leave is if you take something from the zone with you.'

The ghost shrugged and looked at his feet hovering millimetres above the surface of the water. 'Then it looks like I'm stuck here, unless you've got a glass or some other container in your pocket?'

My eyes followed the footpath around the water and

came to rest on a small ornamental bridge at the end of the lake. 'Why don't I meet you there?' I said, nodding towards it. 'I'm sure we can work out a way to get you off the water.'

He smiled unevenly. 'OK, thanks.'

'No worries,' I replied, ignoring the brief flutter in my stomach his gratitude caused. 'It's the least I can do after yesterday. I'm Skye, by the way.'

'Owen Wicks,' he said and then hesitated. 'This is a bit weird, isn't it?'

Now it was my turn to offer a rueful grin. 'Welcome to my world,' I said, shaking my head. 'You get used to it after a while.'

As Owen drifted over the water towards the bridge, I set off along the path. The walk gave me time to think. When I'd first noticed Owen, before the boat had tipped over, I'd wondered what his story was. In fact, I'd been trying to work out whether or not he needed my help. Most people passed straight across to the astral plane when they died, but if their death was tragic or brutal, they were tied to this world until they'd resolved whatever was holding them here. Now that I'd spoken to Owen, it was clear he had no idea what the rules of the afterlife were. I doubted he'd even realised that he wasn't the only ghost around. He needed someone to show him the ropes, make him understand that in some ways death was only the beginning. And it would give me the perfect opportunity to find out what was holding him here, too, not to mention satisfy my curiosity. It was a win-win situation.

Chapter 4

By the time I got to Owen, my inquisitiveness had grown beyond his scar. Whatever the cause, he seemed pretty comfortable with the disfigurement and I wondered how long it had taken him to come to terms with it. Call me shallow, but I couldn't imagine having to adjust to such a life-altering injury. And then there was the whole question of how he'd come to be a ghost on the lake; how could he have drowned with so many people around? But I knew better than to dive in with the heavy questions; the last thing I wanted was to scare him off.

'How long have you been here?' I asked, leaning on the stone parapets and facing away from the rowing boats to block out the memories of the day before.

Owen floated a metre or so above the water, his head level with mine; he'd clearly figured out that the normal rules of gravity didn't apply to the dead. 'A few months, I think. You kind of lose track of time after a while.'

I could see why. Quite often, I woke up wondering what day it was but all I had to do was turn on the TV or radio. Stuck in the middle of the Serpentine, Owen had no access to any of the things the average teenager took for granted. He'd probably sell his soul for an Xbox right now. 'Do you mind if I ask how old you are?'

'Sixteen.' He answered readily enough but I caught the briefest flicker of something behind his eyes, as though he wasn't being completely honest. It was gone before I could work out what it meant and since I couldn't think of a reason he'd lie, I let it go. Besides, there were other things I wanted to know more. The trouble was, I couldn't figure out a way to get any answers without sounding nosy.

Owen took pity on me. 'Look, I know you must have a million questions so why don't we get the basics out of the way? I died by accident, it was my own stupid fault and the scar is completely unrelated. It happened in another accident about six years ago, which was also my fault and, up until a few months ago, the stupidest thing I've ever done,' he said, in a matter of fact tone. Then his mouth twisted ruefully. 'You might guess from this that I am a) accident prone and b) an idiot.'

I couldn't help smiling back. 'Two accidents in sixteen years doesn't sound so bad.'

He shrugged, the smile fading. 'It doesn't really. But here I am. Dead.'

There wasn't much I could say to that. I was quite sure Owen had spent countless hours reviewing the chain of events which had led to his death and wishing he'd done things differently. But if I'd learned anything from hanging around the Dearly D, it was that there was no point in trying to re-roll the dice. Sometimes, the game was over before you were ready.

I looked away then and my attention was caught by a cluster of dried-out bouquets tied to the metal railings beside the bridge. I realised they were there for Owen and my sadness grew. 'Is there anything I can do to help?'

His gaze rested bleakly on me. 'Like what?'

Hugging my arms, I thought back to what my aunt had done for other ghosts. 'I don't know. Bring books, maybe, or a laptop?'

He began to look interested. 'I wouldn't mind catching up with the Grand Prix results. It must be a few races in by now.'

'I could pick up some car magazines for you,' I said, picturing the contents of our coffee table at home and drawing a blank. There was no point in asking Jeremy about fast cars; the closest he'd ever got to speeding was when he'd skidded in the snow in his ancient Nissan Micra.

Owen smiled. 'That would be great. Thanks.'

Returning his smile, I was struck once again by how attractive he was, even with the scar. I'd been focusing on it so hard that I'd forgotten what the rest of his features were like. Now that I was closer to him, I could see that his eyes were grey, the colour of storm clouds in a summer downpour. His eyebrows were thick and brown, like his hair, and he wore a diamond stud in his left ear. I wouldn't mind betting he'd been beating the girls off with a stick before he'd died. 'So I'll come back tomorrow, then? We could go for a walk or something.'

It was quite possibly the lamest suggestion I'd ever made. Owen studied me gravely. 'OK. I'll do you a deal. You bring me up to date with what's happening in Formula One and I'll tell you anything you want to know about me.'

I folded my arms and sniffed. 'I should think so. You did promise to tell me how you got your scar.'

'No, I said it was OK for you to ask about it,' he replied. 'But if you really want to know, I should warn you that it's embarrassing on an epic scale. I might have to kill you if you laugh.'

I bit my lip to smother a smile. 'I'll be the soul of all seriousness.'

'Good,' he said and sounded like he meant it. His gaze was level but once again I caught a flash of something in his eyes and it dawned on me how lonely he must be. 'Same time, same place?'

I nodded, thankful all over again for the freedom the Easter holidays gave me. 'Deal.' I glanced at the lengthening shadows around us. 'It's getting dark. I'd better get going now.'

'Sure,' Owen said. Then he smiled. 'Don't take this the wrong way but I'm really glad you tipped your boat over on the lake yesterday.'

'Me too. Apart from the almost drowning bit, obviously.'

He grinned. 'Obviously. See you tomorrow, then?'

'Yeah. Bye, Owen.'

I was halfway back to Marble Arch when I realised my lips were curving upwards. I was glad I'd met Owen, although the circumstances could have been a little less soggy. As I went down the steps to the Underground, there was one more thing I realised; life had just got a whole lot more interesting.

Something was different in the park the next day. The lake was busy for an overcast Monday afternoon but it wasn't until I reached the bridge that I understood why; propped up against the stone columns and metal railings were bouquets, cards and even a Liverpool FC scarf. Clustered on and around the bridge were small groups of teenagers and adults talking in low voices; occasionally someone kneeled to read a card or adjust the flowers. I hovered on the path, trying to pick out

Owen's distinctive glow but I couldn't see him. The visitors couldn't be marking the anniversary of his death; he'd told me yesterday that he'd only been there a few months. So what was with the flowers and sombre expressions?

Biting my lip, I edged closer. On the one hand, I didn't want to intrude but, on the other, here was an opportunity to get the low-down on Owen. Without meeting anyone's eyes, I approached the mass of flowers and cards and gazed at them in silence.

The bouquets were gorgeous and bright; sunflowers and roses and carnations spilled out of their cellophane wrappings without a lily in sight. There was no sign of the dead flowers I'd noticed the day before. In the centre was a giant seventeen made out of tightly woven red and white carnations and the penny dropped; today would have been Owen's birthday. My gaze slid to the cards. The largest had the words *To a Super Son* picked out in gold letters. Next to it was one which read *Grandson* and there were others to *Friend*, *Cousin* and *Brother*. My eyes grew hot and I felt an abrupt prickling of tears behind them. Suddenly, I didn't want to learn any more about Owen from the tributes lying on the bridge. It felt like I was spying on the misery of the people who had loved him.

I pushed myself upwards and stepped back, ignoring the wave of dizziness caused by standing too quickly.

Stumbling away, I bumped into a girl I hadn't noticed standing behind me. 'Sorry,' I mumbled, shaking away the black dots clouding my vision.

'It's OK,' she replied. Her gaze flickered over me before returning to the flowers and cards. 'Did you know Owen?'

Studying her, I considered my answer. She was taller than me but, since I wasn't what you'd call towering, that didn't mean much. In spite of her height, she looked young and I put her age at around thirteen. Her light-brown hair was pulled back into a ponytail and her eyes were slate grey. There was more than a hint of Owen about her, I noticed; she had to be a relative. 'Not very well,' I admitted, taking care over my words. 'We saw each other around, you know . . .'

She looked at me more closely. 'I don't recognise you from school.'

My stomach tensed. I'd rather not tell an outright lie but, equally, I didn't want to come across as having a ghoulish fascination with the death of someone I didn't know. 'I go to Heath Park C of E, in Highgate,' I said, sticking to the facts and hoping she didn't ask where I'd met Owen. My gaze strayed around the edge of the lake. Where was he, anyway?

Nodding, she said, 'He knew a lot of people. We only found out how many when they couldn't all fit into the church for his funeral.' A sad smile flitted across her face. 'He'd have liked that. Always fancied himself as Mr Popular.'

I thought back to Owen's teasing the day before and his easy charm; I could believe he'd had a lot of friends and I'd bet a lot of them were girls. For a fleeting second, I wondered if he'd left behind a heartbroken girlfriend but it wasn't the kind of thing I wanted to ask.

'His friends said that's the reason he was on the ice in the first place,' the girl went on, glancing out at the lake. 'Showing off to some boys he'd only just met. Maybe if they'd been proper mates they might have stopped him from drinking or stuck around to help him when he fell through, instead of leaving him to drown.'

Her voice was laced with bitterness and tears brimmed on her eyelashes. I didn't know what to say. Part of me was shocked; some of the kids at school were into drinking, stealing from their parents' supplies or fooling shopkeepers into selling them cheap vodka, but I wasn't one of them. My life was complicated enough without throwing in drunken choices. And although Owen had told me he'd drowned in the lake, I hadn't realised it had been frozen at the time. The winter had been mild, until a really cold snap at New Year had ground London to a halt under a flurry of snow and ice. Scotland had been worst hit and I remembered feeling relieved I was no longer facing the ski-slope cobbles and ice-rink steps that Edinburgh's streets became in winter. All of which tied in with Owen's comment that he'd been dead a few months. I couldn't imagine what had possessed him to take such a risk; even if he had been drinking, everyone knew frozen lakes were death traps. Didn't they?

I opened my mouth to mumble something about tragedy when a voice in my left ear made me jump about three centimetres in the air. 'It wasn't their fault. The booze might have kicked in but they did call an ambulance while Max tried to pull me out. It came too late.'

I twisted my head to see Owen behind me, staring at the girl I'd been talking to. He glanced at me and tipped his head in greeting. 'All right? I see you've met my sister.'

So that explained the resemblance. Now that I could compare the two of them, there were other similarities; they both had the same elegantly shaped noses and fine bone structure. I wouldn't mind betting that their mother was stunning and their dad was probably a looker as well.

Aware that the girl was still staring broodingly out at the water, I said, 'I'm sure his friends did their best.'

For a moment, I thought she'd turn all the rage I saw in her eyes on me but then she sighed. 'They said at the inquest that they begged him not to go onto the ice but he wouldn't listen. Typical Owen, he always did like playing Superman. He used to say no one could tell him what to do.'

I glanced at him, to see how he took the comment. He

scowled. 'It was *X-Men*, actually, and at least I didn't grow up thinking I was a Teletubby.'

A snort of laughter escaped me and I hurriedly turned it into a cough. The girl threw me an odd look. 'I should probably go. We're supposed to be having a family party this evening.' Her voice cracked a little. 'Only it won't be much of a celebration without him.'

My heart lurched in sympathy and I wished I could tell her Owen was OK, that he was standing right next to me. It was impossible, though. 'It was nice talking to you,' I said, wondering if I'd see her again. On impulse, I added, 'My name's Skye, by the way.'

The girl eyed me before she answered. 'I'm Cerys. Owen was my older brother.'

'Yeah, I know,' I said, with a wry smile. 'He mentioned you.'

'Really?' Her face brightened. 'What did he say?'

Somehow, I didn't think she'd appreciate Owen's comment about the games she'd played as a kid, but before I could think of a suitable fib, Owen spoke. 'Tell her I said she wasn't a bad kid.'

'He told me you were a great little sister,' I translated, ignoring Owen's loud tut.

Cerys swallowed hard. 'Thanks,' she said after a minute. 'He used to call me a drama queen. I always thought he hated me for stealing Mum and Dad's attention. Maybe I was wrong.'

She flashed me a final brittle smile and hurried towards a group of adults clustered at the end of the bridge. Owen watched her go.

'I did hate her,' he said. 'When I was six, I wanted a puppy and my dad said I couldn't have one because Cerys was too young. And she wet the bed when we went on holiday and blamed it on me.'

Eek. If brotherly love meant having someone to reveal embarrassing facts about you then I was glad to be an only child. 'I bet she worshipped you, though.'

He shrugged. 'I suppose so. Shame I let her down. All of them, really.'

I bit my lip, wanting to reassure him but aware I didn't know him well enough. 'It must be hard, seeing everyone here like this.'

His eyes were bleak as he watched a tall woman with long brown hair reach down to give Cerys a hug. 'It was at first. Straight after I died was the hardest. Mum and Dad were devastated, blamed themselves for not having kept a closer eye on me. I think they found it hard to come here, but Cerys seemed to find some kind of comfort from hanging around. She didn't cry, just talked and watched the water and looked right through me.'

Sometimes I thought the living had it easier than the dead when it came to bereavement. The living lost a loved one but, as painful as that was, at least they had friends and family around to comfort them. The person who'd died was on their own; they'd lost their life, family and friends all at once. The misery in Owen's voice reminded me of how painful and lonely it must have been, watching his family mourn around him. A lump grew in my throat. I swallowed to dislodge it. 'Maybe she could sense your presence.'

Owen shook his head. 'I think she liked watching the birds. Dunno how she didn't get frostbite, actually. My parents couldn't stop her from coming so they used to wait in the café and bring her hot chocolate every now and then.'

I imagined Cerys standing a lonely vigil over the lake and Owen powerless to comfort her. For the second time that day, my heart ached for them. 'There's a place the living and the dead go to talk to each other, through the psychics who work there,' I said slowly, unsure whether I was rushing things. 'It's called the Church of the Dearly Departed. I could tell your sister about it someday, if you wanted? Then you could meet her there.'

Emotion flickered across his face. 'A church full of ghosts?'

'And psychics. As you can imagine, it gets pretty busy.' I watched him absorb the information. 'You did realise there were other ghosts, didn't you?'

He was silent for a moment, then nodded. 'Yeah, of course I did.' His expression changed to one of intense interest. 'So does this mean you've worked out a way to get me off this lake?'

I reached into my pocket and pulled out a smooth round stone I'd plucked from the edge of the lake on my way to the bridge half an hour earlier. 'Happy birthday. Put this in your pocket and you'll be able to go wherever you want. For a while, anyway.'

'How long?' he asked.

'It takes time to build up your ability to stay away,' I explained. 'We'll need to make sure you come back here to recharge after about an hour at first. When you're used to it, you can stay away from your haunting zone for up to twenty-four hours but any longer than that and you get dragged back.' I pulled a face. 'I've heard it's not pretty.'

Owen gazed dubiously at the pebble resting in my palm. 'Right. So how am I supposed to pick it up?'

I wasn't exactly certain of that myself; Mary hadn't been great on the finer details when I'd quizzed her on the suspiciously sharp old letter opener she carried around with her. She'd reassured me that a ghost wouldn't have any problems taking the stone, though.

'It will be one with him and none of the living shall spy it,' she'd intoned in her usual cross-century gibberish. 'But ensure he loseth it not or the lake shall consume him once more.'

I didn't dare ask more in case she realised I wasn't asking about a hypothetical friend at all and mentioned my interest to Celestine. I hadn't said anything about Owen yet; the plan was to introduce him later, once my close encounter with the lake had faded a bit in Celestine's memory.

'I think you just take it,' I told Owen, hoping I didn't sound as uncertain as I felt.

We both stared at my hand for a minute, then Owen squared his shoulders. 'OK. Here goes.'

He reached towards my hand. His fingers slid through mine and wrapped around the stone. When he pulled away, I let out a groan of disappointment. The pebble was still on my palm.

'We must have done something wrong,' I said.

Owen didn't reply. Instead, he turned over his hand and unfurled his fingers. Nestled beside his thumb was an exact clone of the pebble I held. I blinked in confusion. 'How?'

He looked up at me, grinning. 'Don't ask me, you're supposed to be the expert around here.'

My mind whirred as I stared first at my stone, then at Owen's. It made a weird sort of sense, I realised; the stone must exist in both the physical world and in the afterlife at the same time.

'Put it in your pocket and, whatever you do, don't lose it. Believe me, you don't want to be without it when you're not here. You'll get hauled back to where you died before you can blink.'

He tucked it deep into his jeans. 'Safe.' Rubbing his hands together, he smiled at me. 'So, where shall we go?'

I flicked my head towards his family. 'Are you sure you don't want to wait until they've gone?'

'No,' he said, after only the slightest of hesitations. 'It's not as though they know I'm here. Let's go and raise some hell.'

I raised my eyebrows and started to walk towards the path. 'It's your birthday. What did you have in mind?'

Taking a final glance around, Owen followed me. 'I don't mind what we do, as long as it's on dry land. I've had enough water to last me an eternity.'

I thought about that as we left the lake behind us. If I hadn't been sure before that I'd done the right thing in coming back to find Owen, I was now. Without my help to move on, the Serpentine would be his eternity. His future was in my hands.

Chapter 5

'When did you first realise you could see ghosts?'

We were ambling across the grass and Owen was twisting his head this way and that as he drank in the sights everyone else was taking for granted. Top of that list seemed to be me and he wasn't messing about with polite chit-chat.

'I don't actually know,' I admitted, after thinking for a minute. 'They've always been there, for as long as I can remember.'

'Weren't you scared?' he asked, casting an envious glance at a cyclist speeding past. 'I mean, obviously I'm about as terrifying as a kitten on a Christmas card but I'm guessing they're not all like me?'

They weren't and it was probably a very good thing. I was on his right-hand side and kept stealing glances at his profile, finding new things to like about it. In fact, I had to keep reminding myself he was a ghost and not someone I should be feeling in any way attracted to. Developing a crush on Owen would be even more disastrous than my last attempt at a love life, which had begun not long after I'd moved to London and had ended abruptly in a broken heart a few weeks later. I hadn't been able to believe my luck when Nico had asked me out one day at school. Dark-haired and mysterious, he was drop-dead gorgeous and I was – well – different. It had been a fairy tale romance, right up to the moment he'd confessed to being a member of the Solomonarii, an ancient cult from his native Romania, and tried to use me and my gift to contact the dead. His personality had switched from witty and affectionate to sinister and threatening in a heartbeat. I still got the shivers when I thought about the night Nico had chased me through Highgate Cemetery, hammering hailstones and freezing winds down on me as I scrambled to escape him. He hadn't bothered me at school since, and for the past few months, I'd spent each day avoiding him, nursing my broken heart and trying to forget how much I'd cared about him. I wasn't as successful as I'd have liked.

Owen turned an enquiring gaze towards me, catching me in full-on stare mode. All thoughts of Nico melted away as I felt the beginnings of a ruby tide creeping up my neck. I looked away fast and tried to remember what the question had been. 'No, they're not all like you. But I've never been scared – I didn't even realise they were ghosts at first. There was a girl called Poppy who haunted our flat in Edinburgh. My mum thought I was playing with an imaginary friend when I mentioned her.'

Mum had put up with my childish babblings about my 'pretend friend' with good grace, even when I insisted she swapped seats because Poppy wanted to sit next to me. That all changed the day Celestine came to visit, though, and told Mum she could see Poppy, too. We'd moved shortly afterwards and I never saw Poppy again. I wondered about her often, whether she'd understood why I'd abandoned her and found peace. I hoped she had.

Owen threw me a bemused look. 'You really are the weirdest girl I've ever met.'

I shrugged. 'Tell me something I don't know. Weird might as well be my middle name.'

'That would be – uh – weird,' he agreed. 'In every sense of the word.'

I felt a goofy smile threatening to take over my face and cleared my throat. 'Don't think you're going to distract me, by the way. You promised to tell me anything I wanted to know.'

The smile faded from his face. 'So I did. I'm going to regret that, aren't I?'

We were nearing the north-east boundary of the park, where a small crowd was gathered at Speakers' Corner, listening to an elderly man ranting about the little green men who'd stolen his mobility scooter. I gestured to some trees not far away. 'Shall we head that way? This mobile phone earpiece thing gives me some protection but I don't want to end up looking as loony as that bloke.'

Owen nodded and we changed direction. Once we reached the trees, I spread my jacket on the grass and Owen settled down beside me.

'Go on, then,' he said, and I couldn't decide if his grim tone was put on or not. 'What do you want to know?'

I opened my mouth to ask about his scar and closed it again. Maybe he didn't want me to know. He hadn't seemed especially sensitive about it the day before but that could have been bravado. Perhaps he wasn't as OK with it as I'd thought. Besides, another question was oiling its way around my brain and distracting me with its beguiling whisper. I tried to squash it but it was too slippery and had escaped through my mouth before I could stop it. 'Did you have a girlfriend before you died?'

My cheeks flooded with heat and I shut my eyes in mortified horror. Maybe I hadn't really just said that out loud. I opened one eye to see Owen watching me, eyebrows raised in surprise. *Oh God, I had.*

'That wasn't what I was expecting,' he said, lips quirking into a smile. 'But since you ask, I didn't. Girls tended to be scared off by this, believe it or not.'

He pointed to his scar and I felt my face go even redder. He probably thought I was making fun of him. 'Only the shallow ones would have let it bother them,' I said, the words tumbling out, 'and they weren't worthy of your attention.'

Great, now I sounded like his doting grandmother. I resisted the urge to put my head in my hands and groan.

'Thank you,' Owen said gravely. 'I wouldn't have minded a shallow girlfriend. Then at least I would have known what it was like to kiss someone before I died.'

I looked up at him and our eyes met. For a split second something flashed between us and I actually considered leaning forwards and closing the gap between us. Then common sense came crashing in like a tsunami and I clutched at the only support I could find – reality. 'So tell me how you got it.'

Owen eased back a little and grimaced. 'You have to promise not to tell anyone.' He shook his head at me. 'I mean *really* promise. Only my family know the truth.'

Selfishly glad that we seemed to have moved past my embarrassment and onto his, I nodded. 'Psychic's honour.'

He sighed. 'OK. Like I said yesterday, it was about six years ago. Cerys had seen some advert on TV and been bugging Mum and Dad for a pogo stick. So, for her eighth birthday, they got her one. It was pink and played the Go Go Bunnies when you hopped.'

I could practically see it now. And whatever had happened to the Go Go Bunnies? One minute they'd been the world's best-known girlband, the next they'd vanished into pop oblivion, with only a pogo stick to remind the world they'd ever existed. I *might* have danced along to them myself six years ago, although screaming banshees wouldn't have dragged the confession out of me now.

'Anyway, Cerys couldn't get the hang of pogo-ing and soon gave up,' Owen went on. 'Which was when I made my first mistake.'

I was starting to get a sick feeling in my stomach. 'You didn't.'

He pursed his lips and nodded. 'I couldn't resist it. Before long, I was hopping around the garden and it didn't matter that *Shake That Bunny Booty* blasted out with every bounce.'

It was a hysterical mental image but I knew something horrific was coming next. 'Please tell me it wasn't an iron railing,' I whispered, recalling an episode of *Casualty* where someone had impaled their chin on a spiked fence. It hadn't ended well.

Owen pulled a face. 'No, it wasn't that. In fact, I think I'd have been all right if I'd stayed on the grass. But I thought I'd get better air-time if I went onto the concrete. Unfortunately, that's where my dad's greenhouse was.'

I squealed and covered my face. 'Don't. Just don't.'

He puffed out his cheeks. 'I was in hospital for weeks. At one point they were talking about doing a skin graft from my bum. Can you imagine how that would have gone down at school?'

The nicknames didn't bear thinking about. Lowering my hands, I regarded him in sympathy. 'So what did you tell them?'

'That I walked into a glass door. Embarrassing enough but nothing like as bad as it could have been.' He shifted awkwardly on the grass. 'So now maybe you understand why I didn't tell everyone I met?'

I did. 'Thanks for trusting me.'

Owen's smile was both rueful and sad. 'No worries. Who are you going to tell, anyway?'

He was right, of course; who could I tell? Celestine, maybe, but I didn't want her to know about Owen yet. Glancing around the park, I noticed the gathering shadows for the first time. 'I have to go. I'm working at the Dearly D tonight.'

His forehead wrinkled. 'The Dearly D?'

'The Church of the Dearly Departed,' I explained. 'I mentioned it earlier. My aunt is a psychic there and I go along every now and then, to help out with the ghosts.'

He looked away. 'Right. Sounds like fun.'

'It's not as bad as it sounds,' I said, stung by the faint hint of scorn I thought I picked up. 'I'll tell you more about it tomorrow, if you like?'

His eyes met mine. 'You're coming back, then?'

I smirked. 'Of course. If you think for one minute I'm letting you off without at least one chorus of *Shake That Bunny Booty* then you're sadly mistaken.'

He groaned but I thought I caught a glimpse of pleasure in his expression.

'Come on,' I said, clambering to my feet. 'I'll walk you back to the lake. Unless you'd rather bunny hop?'

He rose and shook his head with a mournful expression. 'See? I knew I should have kept my mouth shut.'

Cutting across the park to the tube station, I ran the afternoon's events through my mind. It didn't make entirely comfortable viewing. OK, I'd met Owen's sister and he'd really opened up to me but I'd also come within a cat's whisker of attempting to snog a ghost. Surely that was an abuse of psychic power or something? Celestine would be singularly unimpressed if she knew I was getting emotionally involved with a ghost. My job was to move them on, not give them a reason to stay. I pushed the thought to the back of my mind and hurried towards the tube station, fanning my burning cheeks. I'd just have to make sure no one ever found out about my shameful little fantasy, Owen included. Because one thing was for sure, it wasn't the kind of thing normal psychics went around doing. Even amongst my own kind, I was warped. *Weird* was beginning to sound like the understatement of the year.

Chapter 6

'Have you seen my history textbook? I left it on the dining-room table.'

It was Sunday evening and I was in full-on end-of-holiday panic mode. At the back of my mind was the knowledge that I'd be doing my best not to see Nico at school, but right now I was more concerned with wondering why the contents of my school bag had evaporated the moment I dropped it in the hallway at the end of term. At least I'd finished the witchcraft trials coursework I had to hand in, no thanks to Mary. Muttering dark curses, she'd tried to tip coffee over an illustration of Matthew Hopkins in my history textbook on crime and punishment. In fact, I wouldn't be surprised to discover its torn-out pages stuffed down the toilet. I supposed I couldn't blame her. If I'd been tried as a witch, I'd have been pretty sore at the Witchfinder General, too.

'I realise it's probably a bio-chemical hazard but have you looked in your room?' Jeremy flicked the page of his magazine over and studied the contents. 'I think Celestine took some stuff upstairs earlier when Mary threatened to douse it in candle-wax and burn it like they burned her.'

Eek, I didn't want to think about how I'd explain that one to Miss Pointer at school. I'd already made some ill-advised comments in class and didn't need to draw any more attention to myself. And what did he mean, 'a bio-chemical hazard'? My room might work the lived-in look but it wasn't a landfill site. 'OK, I'll look. Any chance of a lift in the morning?'

Usually, I took the bus but if I was running late then Jeremy dropped me off outside the school gates. Well, I say outside; it depended on who was walking past at the time. Sometimes, I ducked down in my seat and made him drive around the corner so no one saw me getting out of his battered old car.

He shifted on the sofa and threw me an uncomfortable look. 'Sure, if you don't mind taking the scenic route – I'm avoiding Hornsey Lane at the moment.'

I didn't blame him. A few months ago he'd taken me to school and got himself an admirer in the shape of another ghost he could actually see – the suicidal ghost who haunted the bridge on the lane. Despite his best efforts, Isobel had refused to accept that he wasn't interested and now spent most of her time trying to get his attention. Luckily for Jeremy, Mary turned completely hormonal whenever another ghost so much as groaned near our house and Isobel was too scared to come inside, otherwise I had no doubt she'd have stalked him right into the shower. Celestine was being her usual understanding self but even I could see she was rattled by Isobel's misplaced affection. I'd tried everything, from outing Jeremy's secret Barbra Streisand habit to reminding her that his dress sense left a lot to be desired; nothing could persuade her that Jeremy wasn't the one for her and the small fact that he was living and she was dead wasn't going to get in her way.

'I've been thinking about your little problem, actually,' I said.

I had, too, ever since my treacherous subconscious had planted the idea of snogging Owen in my mind. If I needed any more evidence that a living-dead romance was a bad idea, I only had to think of Isobel.

Jeremy looked up. 'Oh?'

'What if she fell for someone else?'

He stared at me. 'Like who? It's not as though she can sign up to Dates-R-Us, is it?'

'No, but there are plenty of single male ghosts at the

Dearly D. Didn't you say your friend Lucy had met her soulmate after she'd died? Why can't Isobel?'

I knew that Lucy had passed across to the astral plane with her ghostly boyfriend, Ryan. Maybe a broken heart was all that was keeping Isobel here; if we fixed that, we'd solve all our problems.

Jeremy opened and closed his mouth several times, as though searching for the downside. Then he said, 'That's not a bad idea. Who did you have in mind?'

Mentally, I flipped through the Dearly D regulars. Isobel was thirty-six and had – well – unusual taste in men, if Jeremy was anything to go by. The church was teeming with male ghosts searching for the meaning of their afterlife – surely one of them would catch Isobel's eye? For one brief second, I considered introducing her to Gawjus George, then dismissed the thought immediately. I couldn't do that to her, no matter how annoying she got; George was older than God and had serious oral hygiene issues. How about Tony, the Elvis impersonator? The white sequinned suit didn't do it for me but he had a good heart and his fake tan wasn't the most orange I'd ever seen.

'I'm still working on that part,' I admitted. 'There must be someone better for her than you, though.'

'Thanks,' Jeremy said, in a dry tone. 'That gives me a real confidence boost.'

Replaying the sentence in my head, I batted him on the arm fondly. 'You know what I mean.'

The corners of his eyes crinkled. 'I do. Thank you.'

'No problem,' I said, sliding onto the sofa and reaching for the laptop. 'I've always fancied myself as a match-maker.'

After a quick Skype call to my mum, I logged onto Facebook to see whether Megan was online. Over a week had passed since our dip in the Serpentine and, although she'd been given a clean bill of health and discharged from hospital, I wouldn't put it past her to use it to escape the first day back at school after the holidays. I'd have probably tried it myself if I thought I could get away with it.

The Friend Request icon in the corner of the screen glowed red at me. I clicked on it, unsurprised when I saw it was from Nico. He'd sent a few requests in recent weeks and I'd ignored them all; it was hard but our break-up had been painful and I wasn't about to risk getting hurt again. Especially since I'd found out the hard way that his love only went as deep as my psychic ability.

Megan wasn't online but she'd messaged me to say she couldn't wait to see Charlie again, which meant nothing short of an earthquake would keep her away from school in the morning. I logged off the laptop, deep in thought. Depending on how my match-making went with Isobel, I might try my hand at getting Megan and Charlie together. Maybe the good karma would bounce back on me and I'd meet a regular boy for a change, someone who wasn't in league with Count Dracula or not breathing any more.

Leaving Jeremy engrossed in his magazine, I trundled up the stairs to look for the history textbook and passed Mary on the landing. She threw me a suspicious look before floating through the ceiling into the attic where she rested. Who was I trying to kid, I asked myself as I closed my bedroom door and surveyed the cluttered floor gloomily. I'd spent the last fourteen years talking to people no one else could see; normal wasn't something that came as standard.

Megan looked like the WAG who'd bagged the footballer when I saw her by the school gates the next morning.

'You're cheerful, considering we've got history this morning,' I commented. 'Did you bang your head when you were underneath that boat?'

She fired a zillion-watt smile in my direction and tucked her arm through mine. 'I don't care. A miracle of epic proportions has happened and not even Miss Pointer's droning voice can burst my bubble of joyfulness today.'

'Wow,' I said, impressed at her level of optimism. 'You really did bang your head.'

Eyes sparkling, she stopped walking and dragged me towards the bushes at the edge of the playground. 'Charlie asked me out!'

Ah. That explained everything. A big grin crossed my face. 'That's awesome! When?'

'Last night. His mum called round to see mine and Charlie came too. We were talking about what movies we wanted to see and I said I liked the look of that new action film that's just come out. So he asked if I wanted to go.' She paused meaningfully. 'With him. As in a date. This weekend.'

I ignored the odd looks her excited squeals were attracting. 'Didn't you tell me you hated the look of that new action movie?' I said, once Megan's noise had subsided. 'I think your exact words were that you'd rather eat live cockroaches than watch it.'

She threw me a mischievous smile. 'Times change. If that's what it takes to get a date with Charlie, then I'm up for the sacrifice. I might even get scared and bury my face in his shoulder and then he can slip his arm around me.'

When it came to romance, Megan was old school, I recalled as we walked to our classroom. I didn't know whether she'd been raised on a diet of Mills and Boon and old films but, in her world, love conquered everything. Even though she'd seen how hurt I was, it had taken a serious amount of persuasion to convince her that Nico and I weren't Highgate's answer to Romeo and Juliet. If I'd told her the truth behind our split, she'd have only been even more convinced we were a pair of star-crossed lovers. I almost felt sorry for Charlie; he had no idea what he'd let himself in for.

* * *

Registration was every bit as dull as always. Ellie MacCauley and her friends sat whispering and firing daggers around the class. Mr Exton droned through the register and tried to stop us from talking, but he might as well have tried to stop the sun from shining. Megan was telling anyone who'd listen about our dramatic afternoon in Hyde Park and I was only mildly miffed when she clasped her hands to her chest and announced that Charlie had saved her life. It was almost a relief to leave her behind and head to my maths class.

The irritation had gone by the time she caught up with me on my way to history. 'You survived maths then?' she said, bouncing along beside me with customary cheerfulness.

We turned the corner into the humanities block and Megan's gaze flickered towards the queue of kids lining the corridor ahead of us.

'So, have you seen You-Know-Who yet?' she asked slyly.

I frowned. 'Lord Voldemort? Funnily enough, I haven't.'

'Ha ha. You know who I mean.'

I guessed she was talking about Nico. 'No, I haven't seen him but since we don't share any of the same lessons, that's hardly a surprise.'

'So it's definitely over between you?'

Gritting my teeth, I counted to ten. 'Once again, that

would be a yes. You saw how messed up I was when we split,' I said, grimacing at the memory. 'There's no chance I'm going through that again. Anyway, he's not interested in me that way.'

Which was sort of true; he might have made me go weak at the knees when he smiled but he'd only been interested in one thing and it wasn't the usual thing boys wanted. After the night in the cemetery, I'd found it hard to believe he'd ever loved me and no amount of wistful sighing by Megan would change my mind.

'Then why is he standing outside our history classroom?' Megan asked, a hint of triumph in her voice.

My gaze shot forwards. Sure enough, Nico was leaning against the wall ahead of us, his tall frame towering over the other kids. I squashed the wave of panicky interest I felt. 'I'm sure it's not because of me.'

Nico's dark eyes felt like dead weights pressing down on me as I forced myself to walk past and joined the end of the line. He didn't speak. Heart pounding, I turned my back and tried to forget he was there, which wasn't easy with Megan switching her attention between us as though she was watching a Wimbledon final. My memory wasn't cutting me any slack, either; I could picture his dark hair curling onto the white collar of his shirt and his mouth curving into a smile. In fact, somewhere deep inside me a sly voice was reminding me exactly how good it had felt to be kissed by him and I realised that, despite my best efforts, I'd never actually forgotten.

'What's he doing here?' I hissed, pushing the thought to one side as Miss Pointer opened up the classroom and Nico filed in ahead of us. 'If this is a joke, it's not funny.'

Scowling as much at my treacherous interest as his presence, I watched Nico slide into the seat directly in front of where I sat. Miss Pointer waited until we'd settled into our usual seats before speaking. 'Good morning, class.'

Wide-eyed, Megan shrugged her shoulders as we mumbled our responses.

'You might have noticed we have a new face with us today,' the teacher went on. 'This is Nico Albescu, who some of you will know from the other half of the year. Due to a timetable switch, he'll be joining this lesson from now on.'

A sick feeling rose up inside me. Was it a simple timetable change, or something else? Maybe I'd been naive to expect he would leave me alone for long. As I stared at the back of his head, he turned to look at me.

'Hello, Skye,' he said, smiling in a way that sent involuntary shivers dancing along my spine. 'Have you missed me?'

Chapter 7

I froze in my seat. In my head, memories flashed past: the first time we'd met, when he'd stopped me from getting a beating; our first date at the Roundhouse; the night I'd trusted him with my secret and that bone-searing moment when he'd turned on me and I'd seen his darker nature. Fists clenched in my lap, I forced myself to meet his gaze.

'Oh yes,' I said, in the most casual tone I could manage. 'Like a cat misses fleas.'

For a nanosecond, I thought I saw a flicker of disappointment on his face but it was hidden before I could be sure. Then Miss Pointer was talking again and Nico turned away to face the front. I let out a shallow sigh of relief.

'Since we have our field trip to the Tower of London

on Friday, I thought it might be good to shake up the usual groups and encourage you to work with new people.' Miss Pointer beamed and waved a brown cloth bag at us. 'So I've put all your names in here and I'll draw them out at random.'

There was a collective groan from the rest of the class but I was feverishly calculating odds. In a class of over thirty kids, what were the chances I'd end up working with Nico?

Unaware of the anxiety she was causing me, Miss Pointer thrust her hand into the bag. 'Group One: Stephan Mitchell, Josie Pickering, Megan Conway and . . .' She paused and rummaged further. 'James Porter.'

Megan threw me a stricken look and I closed my eyes. By the time we'd reached the seventh set of names, I knew with sick certainty that Nico and I would be in the same group. Sure enough, Miss Pointer didn't disappoint.

'Group eight: Ellie MacCauley, Skye Thackery, Amad Patel and Nico Albescu.'

I sank down in my seat, scowling. On a table to my right, Ellie was whispering to her sidekick, looking like she'd just scooped the Euromillions jackpot. I didn't flatter myself it was me she was getting excited about.

Nico twisted in his seat to study me. 'It looks like we're going to be seeing a lot more of each other. I'm glad I switched classes now.'

I didn't reply. Megan kicked me under the table.

'Ow!' I said, reaching down to rub my ankle. 'I've got no intention of seeing any more of you than I have to, Nico. Besides, you're going to have your hands full with Ellie.'

On cue, Ellie fired a bright smile Nico's way. He ignored her and leaned towards me. 'It's not over between us, Skye,' he said, his black gaze pinning me in my seat. 'We'll be doing more than just working together. You'll see.'

Megan's foot banged against my shin again but I barely felt it. Nico had wanted to 'work' with me before, when he'd asked me to help him contact the dead. My refusal had been what sent our relationship into meltdown. Now it seemed he was trying again and using the field trip as cover. The worst of it was that the part of me which still fancied him was happy about it. 'Forget it. I'd rather fail the exam than do anything with you.'

Nico smiled and I felt my stomach flip over treacherously, the way it used to. 'Liar,' he said.

He stared at me for a few more seconds and then faced the front, leaving me to contemplate the back of his head and curse the betrayal of my body. How could I still fancy him after he'd practically kidnapped me? Didn't his involvement with the Solomonarii mean anything? Had I learned absolutely *nothing*?

My head was shouting all these things and more but it was fighting a losing battle. I was attracted to Nico in spite of the danger he posed; maybe even partly because of it. After all, didn't every girl love a bad boy? Fixing my gaze on the desk in front of me, I forced the thoughts away. The best I could do was stay out of his way and try not to be alone with him. Because one thing was obvious; the unofficial amnesty we'd had was at an end.

Megan made it clear she was dying to talk about Nico at lunchtime but that was the last thing I wanted. Instead, I asked her about Charlie and listened with half an ear as she rattled on about the perfect cinema outfit. It wasn't until I noticed her looking at me expectantly that I realised she'd asked me a question.

'Hello, Earth to Skye?' She waggled her hand in front of my face and then grinned. 'Hey, that sounds funny – Earth to Skye.'

'Hilarious,' I said, deadpan. 'You should be on TV.'

She nudged me. 'I thought you'd be happy. Nico definitely wants you back.'

I frowned. 'That's not a good thing. There were reasons why we split up.'

Sniffing, Megan said, 'Probably, but since you've never told me what they were, I can't judge if they were good ones.' She heaved a melodramatic sigh. 'You were so perfect together.'

What could I say? On the outside we did seem perfect for each other: we both loved the same bands, laughed at the same jokes and shared the same values, or so I'd thought. Then he'd ruined everything by asking me to use my gift to help him control the dead and I'd realised how different we really were.

'Trust me, you'd have done the same.'

She didn't look convinced. 'So there's no chance of a double-date any time soon?'

I rolled my eyes; would she never give up? 'Not even if my life depended on it,' I told her, folding my arms in a gesture of finality. 'It's over. Finished. Dead and buried.'

She took the hint and changed the subject. I relaxed a bit, relieved that she'd let it drop, and tried to convince myself that my feelings for Nico really had died that night in Highgate Cemetery. Except I knew better than anyone that the dead had a way of making their presence felt.

Chapter 8

I was willing to try just about anything to take my mind off Nico's reappearance in my life. So when Owen told me he wanted to go to Leicester Square for the première of a new movie he'd heard some kids talking about, I gave it some serious thought. It might be crowded and I doubted we'd get close to the hot blond actress Owen was keen on, but at least I'd be too busy being jostled to think about Nico. Then reality kicked in. Conversation with Owen would be impossible – there was only so much protection my mobile phone earpiece could give me. Besides, as any psychic in London soon discovered, Leicester Square was home to a whole host of unusual ghosts. From wannabe film stars to long dead buskers, they were all drawn to the bright lights and vibrant atmosphere. And then there was Lenny, the resident ghostly flasher. He'd yanked his grubby raincoat open in my face once before and it wasn't an experience I wanted to repeat, not even in the interests of forgetting Nico.

'Why don't you come to my house for a while?' I said, when Owen refused to listen to my reasons for avoiding Leicester Square. 'I bet they'll be covering the première on the local news and they will probably show some clips of the film.'

Grumbling, he agreed. It wasn't until we'd cleared the crowds on Archway Road that something occurred to me.

'We'll need to be careful,' I warned. 'Mary will be out at her coven meeting but, if you're there when she gets back, all hell will break loose. Seven shades of it, in fact.'

Owen looked at me blankly. 'Who is Mary? And what's a coven meeting?'

I hesitated. On paper, Mary sounded pretty terrifying; I mean, who wouldn't be scared by a raggedy five-hundred-year-old ghost who made the Wicked Witch of the West seem like a saint? Once you got past her prickly exterior, though, Mary was actually OK. Unless you were another ghost and she thought you were muscling in on her territory. Then she'd invoke the mysterious covenant she'd signed with my great-grandparents to ensure she was the only spook to haunt their house. At first, I'd assumed Celestine was only humouring her to keep the peace but I'd learned that there could be some pretty horrific results if Mary chose to use the covenant. Rivers of blood seeping down our walls would only be the start.

'She's the ghost who haunts our house,' I explained, 'and on Monday nights, she's a practising witch. Let's just say she's not really a people person.'

The house was quiet when I slid my key out of the lock and pushed the front door open. There was no sign of Isobel lurking opposite and I guessed she'd be at the theatre, trying to catch Jeremy's eye as he worked.

'Hello? Anyone home?' I held my breath as my voice bounced back to me. After listening for a few seconds, I let out a sigh of relief. 'Come on, I'll give you the tour.'

I turned to Owen but he wasn't there. Instead, he was in the living room, staring at the flat screen TV with a hungry expression. Shaking my head, I followed him. I might have known it would catch his eye; how long had it been since he'd watched telly?

'Or we could just watch the television,' I offered, reaching for the remote. We'd timed it perfectly; the presenter had covered all the serious stuff and was onto the entertainment news. Owen and I settled on the sofa and, within minutes, the première crowds were on-screen and a reporter was thrusting her microphone into the faces of the stars.

'Just think,' Owen said, gazing with admiration at the face of the lead actress. 'I could have got close enough to touch her. How awesome would that have been?'

'Pretty awesome,' I agreed, trying to keep an

inexplicable edge from creeping into my voice. 'Except that unless she's a psychic, she wouldn't have actually known you were there.'

He gave an absent nod and watched until the reporter cut back to the studio. Then he turned to me. 'Right. What else is on?'

I ought to have asked him to go; he wasn't practised enough to spend hours away from the lake yet. But he looked so comfortable that I didn't have the heart. And if I was being honest with myself, I didn't really want him to leave; I was enjoying sitting beside him on the sofa. Grabbing the TV listings magazine, I flipped to the right page. 'Let's see, we've got *Coronation Street* on ITV, *EastEnders* later on the BBC or *Hollyoaks* over on Channel Four.'

He gave me a level stare. 'All my favourite shows, how did you know?'

I grinned. 'Lucky guess. Actually, you've missed *Hollyoaks*. It was on earlier, sorry. Did you have anything in particular in mind?'

I thought he'd ask me to flip to the sports channels but I was wrong.

'Is *Top Gear* on?' he said, peering at the magazine in my hands. 'There's always a repeat on one of the channels and I wouldn't mind drooling over a decent set of wheels.' His eyes gleamed. 'Or better still, have you got an Xbox?'

Thankfully, we didn't or he'd have been taking up

permanent residence. Sticking around for half an hour was one thing; getting stuck into *Call of Duty* was another. Besides, although ghosts could learn to move objects in the physical world, it took practice and I didn't want to know how long it would take to work the controller of a games console. Weeks, probably, by which time we'd be knee-deep in cockroaches, thanks to Mary's covenant.

'No,' I said, casting an uneasy glance over my shoulder as though Mary was behind me. 'On second thoughts, maybe we should watch the TV in my room. It's not as big as this one but it's safer in case Mary comes home early.'

Drooping like a toddler who'd had his toy truck taken away, Owen followed me into the hallway and up the stairs. Too late, I remembered the mess I'd left my room in that morning. 'Excuse the stuff on the floor,' I said, as I pushed the door back and kicked a pile of discarded clothes out of the way. 'Mary is a bit of a poltergeist on the quiet.'

His mouth quirked. 'Right. So it's not that you're chronically messy or anything?'

I pretended to be hurt. 'No. I'm Little Miss Tidy normally.'

'Shame,' he said, peering at a pile of books next to my bed. 'If death has taught me anything, it's that life is too short to hoover a bedroom.'

I felt the same way but, unsurprisingly, my aunt didn't. Every now and then, she'd send me upstairs armed with a black bin liner and instructions to decontaminate the carpet. But she was much more relaxed than my mum had been. In Mum's world, dust was the enemy, not something to doodle in.

Smoothing the duvet across the bed, I sat down and scanned the room for the TV remote. Owen sat next to me, looking around.

'Hey, you've been to see The Droids!' Owen exclaimed, pointing towards the ticket from the Roundhouse in Kentish Town I'd pinned to my wall. 'On a scale of one to ten, how amazing were they?'

I thought back to that night, which had been stand-out in all kinds of ways. That had been before I'd discovered the real reason for Nico's interest in me, when I'd still thought he liked me for me. 'They were brilliant,' I replied, picking my words with care. 'It's a fab venue, too.'

My mixed feelings must have been obvious because Owen said, 'I've brought back bad memories. Sorry.'

'That's OK.' I pulled a face, half-impressed he'd picked up on my underlying emotions. 'I went with my ex and we – uh – broke up a few weeks later.'

He studied me. 'But you still have the ticket on your wall so it can't have been all bad.'

What could I say? The time Nico and I had spent

together had been the best weeks of my life; right up until he'd spilled about the Solomonarii and expected me to be impressed. And the weeks after it had been the worst I'd ever known. It summed up our relationship perfectly: divine highs and hellish lows. If I needed another reminder to stay away from him at school, here it was.

I forced a smile. 'Like I said, the band was great. I've got their album on my laptop. Hang on.'

Opening up my laptop, I started up iTunes and chose a playlist. The sound of The Droids' grimy baseline filled the room. Owen took the hint and let the subject drop. Instead, he gazed wistfully at the laptop. 'I miss being online. Would it be morbid to ask you to log into Facebook for me? It'd be good to see what my mates are up to.'

A jolt of realisation ran through me; I hadn't even thought that he'd have an account but of course he must have. Everyone did. But the idea of bringing Owen's page up on screen made me uneasy. It was common for Facebook accounts to remain open after the owner had died, so that friends could write messages on the wall and remember the good times together. If Owen logged into his account, who knew what he might see?

'That would mean telling me your password,' I said slowly. 'Can't I just search for you instead?'

He shook his head. 'We weren't friends, you won't be able to see anything.' A smile tugged at his lips. 'Don't worry, I trust you not to write anything rude on my wall.'

That wasn't what he needed to worry about; his family would be sure to see whatever I wrote and I knew better than to mess with their grief. What I didn't know was whether I could trust myself not to spy on his life; I'd hate it if someone nosed around the dodgy tagged pictures on my profile. If I had his password, I'd be able to see everything, from those photos to his inbox. Would I be able to resist checking out what kind of boy he'd been before he died?

'I have a better idea,' I said, pushing the thought aside. 'Why don't I introduce you to one of the secrets of the afterlife?'

He looked puzzled. 'OK.'

'What we need is your finger, some determination and something to practise with.' Grabbing a piece of paper from my bedside table, I scrunched it into a ball. 'Ready?'

Still eying me with uncertainty, he nodded. Grinning, I dropped the paper ball onto the keyboard and slid it towards him. 'Trust me. You're going to love this.'

An hour and a half of frustrated shouting and the occasional rude word later, he was just starting to get the hang of it. Some ghosts never summoned up enough emotion to move objects in the physical world. Others, like Mary, used their internal rage and were masters of smashing ornaments. They took great delight in hiding the everyday things the living took for granted, like shoes and keys. Or toothbrushes, in my case. It wasn't an easy thing for ghosts to learn how to do but, once they had, it opened up a lot of possibilities.

'Are you sure I need to be able to do this?' he asked, as his finger passed through the ball and into the keyboard once more.

'Do you want to log into Facebook or not?' I answered, flicking the ball up in the air. 'Dontay told me this is the hardest bit, honestly.'

'Dontay?'

I reached around him to grab the paper, careful not to lean in. I knew most ghosts hated people passing through them, even though the living rarely felt much more than a shiver down their spine, as though someone had walked over their grave. 'A friend of mine. He passed across to the astral plane a few months ago.'

Owen watched me for a moment, then aimed his outstretched finger at the ball I'd placed back on the keyboard. 'Not the one you went to see The Droids with?'

'No. Dontay was a ghost and —' I wanted to say that it would have been stupid to fancy a ghost but, sitting there with Owen, it didn't seem stupid at all. My crush on him wasn't going away; if anything it was getting worse. 'We were just mates.'

At that second, he connected with the paper and it tumbled onto the bed beside me.

'Hey, you did it!' I cried, beaming at him. 'See? All you had to do was find the right emotion.'

He stared at the ball. 'Again.'

I replaced it in front of him and his face creased in concentration as he poked at it. As before, it rolled off the keyboard.

'What you need to do now is find something to practise on,' I said, picking the paper up and placing it on my outstretched palm. 'The lake should have plenty of litter around, even if it is a bit waterlogged.'

His finger stabbed at the ball and it flew off my hand. Then I felt the lightest of tickles on my palm as his fingertip brushed my skin. It was gone almost instantly but one look at Owen told me he'd felt it too.

'You touched me!' I breathed.

His eyes locked onto mine. 'Did that really just happen?'

'I think so.' Scrabbling for the paper ball, I put it on my hand. He poked his finger towards it, slower and more controlled than before. The ball toppled onto the duvet and I felt the graze of his finger again. This time, instead of a feathery light whisper, I felt a cool pressure and he didn't lift it away. Then the sensation vanished and I realised he'd let go.

I blinked at him. 'How did you do that?'

'I don't know. Haven't you ever touched a ghost before?'

I shook my head. Apart from that moment in the park

where I'd imagined kissing him, the idea had never crossed my mind before. Wait a minute . . . my eyes slid guiltily to his mouth and I couldn't quite believe what I was thinking. If his finger could touch my hand then surely his lips would be able to brush mine?

'Skye?' Owen asked, as my hands flew to cover the crimson blush racing across my cheeks. 'What's wrong?'

Mortified, I couldn't look at him. 'Nothing. I'm fine.'

He dipped his head until his eyes met mine. 'Did I do something I shouldn't?'

'No!' The word shot out of me. 'I'm the one with the problem.'

'Right. And what problem is that?'

I didn't answer. Owen watched me in silence for a minute, then asked, 'Does it have something to do with whether or not I had a girlfriend?'

I closed my eyes. This was a nightmare. It was bad enough when someone found out you fancied them but, when you knew your feelings were completely inappropriate, it was a zillion times worse.

Owen was waiting for me to reply. Reluctantly, I opened my eyes and looked at him. 'Maybe.'

A faint smile tugged at the corners of his mouth. 'Good,' he said and leaned closer towards me. 'Because I like you, Skye. And I don't see why the living should get to have all the fun.'

I stared into his gunmetal eyes. Now that I was really

close to him, I could see tiny flecks of gold around the iris of each one and long golden lashes framing them – so different from Nico's dark, intense stare. Mesmerised, I gazed at Owen as we edged closer together and a sense of unreality stole over me. Were we actually going to try this? Was I really about to kiss a ghost?

For the first few seconds, I wasn't sure if our lips were touching. But then I felt it: a soft fluttering, like the silken brush of butterfly wings against my mouth. It was the strangest, most sensuous feeling I'd ever experienced and completely unlike any kiss I'd had before. It teased the nerve-endings in my lips, making them tingle as the blood pulsed through them. I leaned into Owen, seeking more contact, and raised my hand to cup his cheek. It wasn't until my fingers met thin air where they expected skin that I opened my eyes and the full enormity of what we were doing hit home.

Then the door of my room opened. Owen and I jerked apart to see Jeremy framed in the doorway. I sagged with shame-faced relief; I'd expected it to be Celestine, and at least Jeremy couldn't see Owen.

'Sorry to barge in, Skye,' he said. 'I did call out but I don't suppose you heard me over the music.'

Yeah, I thought, or over the roar of my own raging hormones. Forcing myself to breathe normally, I swallowed. 'It's OK.'

Jeremy frowned. 'Warm in here, is it?' he asked, giving

me a long appraising look. 'You should open the window, you look a bit flushed.'

He started to pull the door closed and Owen and I exchanged relieved glances. Then Jeremy stopped and poked his head into the room. 'By the way, if you're going to start bringing friends up here, we should probably set some ground rules.' He looked straight at Owen and dropped him a knowing wink. 'Ghostly or not, boys will be boys!'

Chapter 9

I thought I would actually die of embarrassment. If you'd asked me, I couldn't have told you which was worse; Jeremy's toe-curling hint that something was going on between me and Owen, or the shameful knowledge that he wasn't a million miles from the truth. A groan of mortification escaped me. I didn't want to think about what might have happened if he'd walked in a few seconds later.

'I thought you said he wasn't psychic,' Owen ventured, once the door had closed on Jeremy's self-satisfied chuckling.

I gritted my teeth. 'No, I said he was part psychic, although I'm beginning to wonder if that was all an act just to catch me out. He isn't normally home this early, either.'

Owen grimaced. 'Well, he definitely knew I was here.'

Which meant that pretty soon Celestine would know and I'd have some explaining to do. And that left me with a dilemma; how much should I tell her? That Owen had helped me at the lake and nothing more, or confess how close I was to crossing the line between the acceptable and the downright wrong?

'You should probably go,' I said out loud, checking the time on the laptop. 'Mary will be back soon and you've met quite enough of my family for one night.'

He stood up and stretched. 'Thanks for letting me come over. I had fun.'

'That's OK,' I said, trying not to wonder what would have happened if Jeremy hadn't interrupted. 'I don't invite many people here, for obvious reasons.'

'I can see how it might be a bit awkward,' Owen agreed. His eyes strayed to the laptop. 'I suppose I'll have to wait to log into Facebook.'

I got to my feet and smiled encouragingly. 'At least now you can. If you spend a bit of time practising then you'll have no problems using the track-pad next time you come over. If you wanted to come over again, I mean.'

'I'll try,' he said. 'Thanks for sharing the secret with me. You know, how to touch things.'

I felt myself start to go red as I thought about what he'd actually touched. 'No worries,' I said, willing my cheeks to cool down. 'Happy to help.'

He paused to look at me and I wondered if he was

going to mention our kiss. Then his gaze skittered away. 'So I'll see you soon, then?'

Nodding a bit too fast, I replied, 'Absolutely. I'll pop by the lake after school on Thursday, bring some magazines.' Then my brain seemed to switch off and my mouth took on a life of its own. 'Shall we go and see that film at the weekend?'

Owen's face lit up. 'Yeah, OK. As long as you let me sniff your popcorn.'

I grinned. 'I think that could be arranged.'

'So it's a date, then.' He smiled and my stomach went *zoing*. 'I'm looking forward to it already.'

After he'd gone, I looked him up on Facebook. As he'd guessed, his account was protected and I couldn't see anything except his name and his profile picture. It had been taken on some kind of race track – there was a chequered flag in the background and he was laughing into the camera. I could barely make out his scar but the tell-tale twist of his mouth gave it away. On impulse, I clicked on the Friend Request button. Someone in his family was probably maintaining the account and, with a bit of luck, it might be Cerys so I could talk to her. If I wanted to figure out why Owen was still here, I'd need to find out more about him without crossing the line into snooping. And whether I liked it or not, at the back of my mind was the memory of our ghostly kiss. It had been the sweetest and the most frustrating snog of my life;

almost real but not quite. I was looking forward to our date at the cinema; Owen was the perfect way to distract myself from Nico. Maybe – just maybe – we'd find a way to make our next kiss good enough to blow my attraction to Nico away forever.

By the time Thursday afternoon rolled around, the mere thought of history made me feel like throwing up. My attempts to get out of the field trip had fallen on deaf ears with Celestine, even when I played my trump card and mentioned Nico, and I knew it was because of the row we'd had over Owen.

'Of course nothing was going on,' I'd lied when she'd raised the subject with me at the Dearly D on Tuesday evening.

'That's not what Jeremy said,' she'd fired back, smiling at old Mrs Chester as she tottered through the pews in front of us. 'He said you were all over each other.'

'I was helping Owen learn how to touch things, that's all,' I answered, making a mental note to have a quiet word with Jeremy about his tabloid tendencies. 'The same as I did with Dontay.'

She'd scowled. 'I don't remember having to prise you and Dontay apart. You knew the rules back then.' Pausing, she'd lowered her voice. 'I'm sure I don't have to remind you that getting emotionally attached to a ghost is a sure-fire path to misery. When he passes across – and that's what you're supposed to be helping him to do, remember – you'll both end up broken-hearted.'

I'd opened my mouth to reply and closed it again. I had nothing. She was one hundred per cent right. It didn't mean I had to like it, though.

'Break it off, Skye,' she commanded. 'Better still, get him to come here so that one of the other psychics can help him. Don't give him a reason to stay here longer than he needs to. It's not fair.'

In the end, I'd agreed to her demand but it had been grudging and she knew it. So she hadn't been exactly receptive when I'd asked for a letter excusing me from history. She'd argued that I'd have to face up to Nico one day and it was better to do it in a public place like the Tower of London than somewhere quiet and isolated. Never mind that there was more chance of running into a ghost there than pretty much anywhere else in London.

My hope that Nico would have been struck down by any passing disease came to nothing either; he was waiting in line outside the classroom, his black gaze fixed on me as I pretended not to notice him. Once we were in our seats, the lesson went immediately downhill.

'You're going to be looking at source material today, ahead of tomorrow's trip. Split into your working groups and discuss the images on the sheets I'm handing round.'

Scraping her chair back, Megan waggled her eyebrows at Nico's back as she looked at me. I sighed.

Ellie had made her way to Nico's side at warp speed. 'I was thinking that we could be partners and give these two losers the push,' she said, flicking her dark hair over her shoulder and smiling flirtatiously down at him. I rolled my eyes at Amad, who pushed his glasses up his nose nervously and hugged his exercise book to his chest.

Nico swivelled around in his chair to face me. 'You're making it too easy, Ellie,' he said. 'You should play hard to get, like Skye here. It's much more alluring.'

I snorted. 'Or impossible to get, even.'

'You weren't always.' Nico leaned towards Ellie and lowered his voice confidentially. 'She pretends to hate me but it's all a front.'

Summoning up my most disinterested expression, I pulled Megan's empty chair out from under the table and pointed to it. 'Take a seat, Amad. It looks like we're the only ones who'll be getting any work done in this group.'

'Wouldn't you rather sit here, Ellie?' Amad asked, his voice a mixture of awed hesitancy and adoration.

'Drop dead, pond scum,' Ellie snapped, without even a glance, slamming her books on the table and stalking around to perch on the only other available seat, next to Nico.

Amad crumpled into the seat. 'O-OK. No problem.'

'See?' Nico grinned at Ellie and raised a wolfish eyebrow. 'You're learning already.'

When it came down to it, Nico worked harder than I

expected. While Ellie didn't even pretend to look at the letters and images we'd been given to interpret, Nico mostly ignored her blatant flirting and came up with some insightful comments about punishment through the ages. My heart sank when we got to the last question, however.

'*Using sources 4A to 4D, give a variety of reasons someone might be tried for witchcraft in sixteenth-century England and explain how punishment for the crime changed over time*,' Nico read.

His eyes locked onto mine. Steeling myself, I waited for the inevitable jibe but it wasn't Nico who made it.

'God, this is so boring,' Ellie burst out. 'Who cares why a bunch of attention-seeking freaks got what was coming to them? It's not like witchcraft actually exists, anyway.'

Nico and I looked away. 'It doesn't matter whether the accusation was accurate,' I said in a careful tone. 'What matters is how unfairly they were treated.'

'You would take their side,' Ellie snapped back at me, her mouth twisted in disgust. 'You're even weirder than they were. I bet if you'd been alive back then, they'd have burned you at the stake, too.'

'You should have a bit more respect, Ellie,' Nico said and I thought I caught a glitter of amusement in his eyes. 'If Skye really was a witch, she might turn you into something even nastier than you already are.'

Ellie looked like she'd been slapped. 'She's really sucked you in, hasn't she? Don't tell me you believe in all that hocus-pocus crap?'

Nico was very still. He tilted his head and studied Ellie intently. 'Never walked into a room and had the prickling feeling someone else just left?' he said, his voice low and mesmeric. Outside the window, the sky had darkened to an ominous grey and the light in the classroom seemed suddenly inadequate. The hubbub of the other kids faded. 'Or lain there in bed at night and wondered if that creaking noise on the stairs is really just the floorboards? Never walked through a silent graveyard in the dark and prayed that the dead stay that way?'

Ellie was doing her best to ignore him but I could see he was getting to her. Amad kept his head down and looked like he might burst into tears. 'We've only got ten minutes left to finish this.'

Leaning closer to Ellie, Nico stared into her eyes. 'Haven't you ever been home on your own and been sure there was someone creeping up behind you? But when you spun around, heart thumping, there was no one there?'

On cue, a crack of thunder rattled the windows and a flash of lightning lit up the sky. Ellie and half the rest of the class screamed, then let out sheepish laughter as they looked at each other. Chatter broke out amongst the groups.

'You're as much of a freak as she is,' Ellie said, tossing her hair over one shoulder in shaky disdain. 'I don't know what I ever saw in you.'

Nico leaned back in his seat. 'Mission accomplished.'

Miss Pointer's voice rose above the noise of conversation. 'Pack your things away now. Don't forget, you'll need a packed lunch tomorrow and make sure you're wearing full school uniform. Anyone going plain clothes will be thrown into the dungeons.'

Groans rang out around the room. Stuffing her books into her bag, Ellie sneered at me. 'I don't know what kind of spell you've cast on him.'

I smiled my sweetest smile. 'I thought you didn't believe in all that hocus-pocus.'

She scowled. 'Just stay away from me tomorrow, both of you. Amad, make sure you bring a notebook in the morning. You're going to be doing my work for me.'

Looking like all his birthdays had come at once, Amad scooped up his notes and nodded. Ellie fired a final withering glare my way and stormed off, with Amad scurrying behind her like a bespectacled Gollum from *Lord of the Rings*.

'You're welcome,' Nico said, when it became clear I wasn't going to thank him.

'What for?' I asked, getting to my feet and swinging my bag over my shoulder. 'Making Ellie hate me even more than she already did?'

He grinned, and my lunch flipped over lazily inside me. 'I thought you needed defending. Besides, if it's any consolation, she hates me too, and at least we can get on with our work in peace tomorrow.'

I stared at him. 'You did it on purpose.'

'Did I?'

Suspiciously, I glanced out of the window. There was no sign of the thunderous clouds now; the playground was bathed in late afternoon sunshine. I lowered my voice to a whisper. 'Was that you messing with the weather?'

Nico shrugged. 'It added to the sinister atmosphere, I thought.' Waving the source documents Miss Pointer had given us, he said, 'We should finish this before tomorrow. Want to go to the library after school?'

Megan was weaving her way towards me and her eyes took on an extra gleam when she saw the two of us talking. 'No, I'm busy. And don't get any ideas about tomorrow, Nico. We go, we do the work, we come back.'

He shrugged. 'Whatever you say.' Leaning towards my ear, he whispered, 'But I'm sure we'll be alone at some point in the Tower. Then maybe I can prove that I'm not who you think I am.'

He leaned down further and grazed his lips against my ear and then he was gone. Gripping the table, I steadied myself against the storm of tingling his touch had caused. Seconds later, Megan appeared next to me.

'Oh my God!' she squeaked, her eyes wide. 'Did he really just kiss your ear?'

My cheeks began to burn and I hurriedly summoned up an image of Owen in an effort to squash my treacherous feelings. 'I'm sure it was an accident.'

Megan nodded. 'Of course it was. Like when he *accidentally* snogged you in the hallway in front of half the year.'

Fanning my face, I made my way out of the classroom. 'Leave it, Megan.'

She followed me, determined to make her point. 'Face it, Skye, Nico is into you big time.' A wise expression crossed her face and she wagged a finger in my direction. 'You guys are so going to get back together.'

'Over my dead body!' I snapped, then gulped. Thinking back over what I knew of the Solomonarii, I knew they were ruthless in their pursuit of power. I didn't think Nico wanted to hurt me but the rest of the clan was a different matter. Exactly how far were they prepared to go to get what they wanted?

Chapter 10

I tried to put Nico's parting comment out of my head as I travelled to Hyde Park. More than that, I tried to push away the memory of his touch and the way it had made me feel. But then the knowledge of what I had to do when I arrived at the Serpentine re-emerged and that wasn't a brilliant thought, either. Shaking my head, I buried my headphones further into my ears and turned up my iPod. My love life was a joke. First Nico, now Owen; it really was about time I found myself a normal boyfriend, who was actually alive and didn't demand that I contacted the dead for him.

It wasn't a bad spring evening and the park was busy. The flowers from Owen's birthday were gone but the Liverpool scarf was still tied to the railings, its tassels grubby and weathered. As I watched, a dog trotted up and cocked its leg against it.

'Obviously a Chelsea supporter,' Owen said behind me, making me jump. I'd had the uneasy feeling someone had been watching me all the way from the underground station but had put it down to Nico's games with Ellie earlier. Now I guessed it must have been Owen.

'It's rude to sneak up on people.'

He raised a surprised eyebrow. 'Hello to you, too.'

I sniffed. 'There's no need to follow me around.'

A frown creased his forehead. 'I didn't. I saw you walking across the grass and came over to speak to you.'

Throwing him a searching look, I decided to give him the benefit of the doubt and sighed. 'Sorry. I think I'm a bit touchy.'

'Bad day?'

I considered letting the truth spill out of me; that my ex, who just happened to be involved with an evil clan which took unsuspecting ghosts and turned them into shadowy undead servants, wanted me to help him with his monstrous plans. Unsurprisingly, I thought better of it. 'You could say that.'

'Did you bring any more magazines?' he asked.

I nodded. 'Want to find somewhere to sit down and read? I'll turn the pages for you.'

'Maybe I'll turn them myself,' Owen replied. 'I've been practising.'

We found a tree to sit under and worked our way

through the glossy articles. Owen was right; he had been practising, although he wasn't good enough to grip the slippery pages yet. I tried to listen as he explained who the drivers were in each photograph but Celestine's words kept floating to the front of my mind. I should be helping him to move on instead of giving in to my own selfish feelings, no matter how much I wondered about kissing him again.

I cleared my throat. 'What did you do today?'

Owen laced his fingers behind his head and lay back on the grass. 'Not much. Followed Cerys to school, checked in on my mum and dad.' His lips curved into a smile. 'Saw a wicked Ferrari on the way back and caught up on the footie scores from an abandoned paper. And that's pretty much it, unless you count skimming a flattened Coke can over the lake.'

'You must get really bored.'

'I used to. You wouldn't believe how hard it is watching people getting on with their lives, doing all the things you'll never be able to again. Things aren't so bad now I can move around, though.' He squinted up at me, his smile widening. 'And then there's you.'

His smile was contagious, in spite of knowing what I had to do. Was it really so wrong to want to be friends with Owen, to get to know him before the opportunity was gone? I'd done the same with Dontay, after all. But inside, I knew that the comparison was flawed. Dontay had been a mate and nothing more; I'd never lost sight of the ultimate goal and I'd certainly never day-dreamed about snogging him. With Owen, the goalposts kept shifting and I knew it was because my emotions were making everything cloudy and Nico wasn't really helping. It wasn't fair on either Owen or me and, no matter how much I wished things were different, I had a duty to stop it from happening.

Digging my nails into the palms of my hands, I tried to sound casual. 'There's a service at the Dearly D tonight and my aunt wants me to help out. I wondered if you fancied keeping me company?'

The contented expression he wore faded. 'Will there be loads of other ghosts?'

I nodded. 'All the usual suspects, plus a few new ones. I can even introduce you to Jeremy's stalker, if you like.' Pausing nervously, I licked my lips. 'My aunt wants to meet you, too.'

He went still. 'Your aunt? Why?'

'Don't worry, she's not going to exorcise you. Jeremy told her about you and she's interested, that's all.'

Uncertainty played across his face. 'I don't know . . .'

'Please,' I said, my fingers twitching with the urge to take his hand. 'I promise she's not scary and it'll be good for you to meet other ghosts. Even if one of them is Gawjus George. Maybe someone will pass across, it'd be good for you to see.'

Owen studied me dubiously. 'What do you mean, pass across?'

Making it sound as unscary as I could, I explained. When I'd finished, he looked less than keen on the idea. 'Honestly, it's nothing to be afraid of.'

Sitting up, he refused to look at me. 'That's easy for you to say. All this stuff is new to me. You don't have it hanging over you.'

'True,' I replied and my heart thumped uncomfortably in my chest. 'But I might someday.'

He snorted. 'When you're old and have actually done something with your life. I wasn't ready to die and I'm not ready to give everything up yet.' His hands clenched into fists at his sides. 'There's so much I still want to do, make sure my family is all right, for a start. I don't want to leave you, either.'

I stared at him and realisation dawned. Bubbling underneath his calm exterior was a seething anger that he'd died so young. No wonder he wasn't interested in going to the Dearly D; he was still clinging to his old life. Why hadn't I seen it before? Then another thought occurred to me. Was that the reason we'd ended up kissing on Monday night? Maybe he saw me as another way of holding onto everything he used to have.

'You won't go until you're ready,' I said quietly, resisting the temptation to reach out towards him. 'Look at Mary, she's been here five hundred years or so and we still can't get rid of her. Not that I'm suggesting you do the same.'

Some of his agitation drained away. 'It's so hard. I miss everything.' He let out a ragged sigh. 'My family, my mates, racing around the go-kart track, quad biking, watching Liverpool win at Anfield. Sometimes I even miss the way rain used to feel on my skin, if you can believe that?'

The longing on his face was painful to see. A lump grew in my throat. I swallowed and tried to lighten the mood. 'Yeah. You probably don't miss Marmite, though.'

He threw me an incredulous look. 'Are you kidding? It's in my top ten of things I miss. Marmite on toast is a god amongst foods.'

I grimaced in an effort to distract him. 'How can you say that? It's a well-documented fact that the Spanish Inquisition invented it to torture their prisoners with.'

To my relief, some of his awful tension eased. We argued good-naturedly for a few minutes before agreeing to disagree. Then I glanced at my watch. 'So what do you think? Want to come and meet the family?'

He considered the question so long that I was sure he was going to turn me down. Then he shrugged. 'OK. But at the first sign of sparkly lights, I'm out of there. My name's not Edward Cullen.'

* * *

There wasn't time to head home before I was due at the Dearly D so I texted Celestine to say I'd meet her there. Besides, I didn't want to risk running into Mary; meeting my aunt was going to be scary enough without throwing a witch with territorial tendencies into the mix. Owen suggested we caught the street entertainment in Covent Garden and we whiled away some time sitting on the pavement in a quiet corner, watching the silvery human statues pose for the crowds and a fire-eater mesmerise the tourists.

Kensal Green made a stark contrast to the flashy delights of the West End. I didn't wear my hands-free earpiece so I couldn't speak to Owen much; Jeremy had warned me not to look like I had anything worth stealing. The skin between my shoulder blades itched as we threaded our way through the dusk-filled streets and I cast frequent uneasy glances over my shoulder to see if we were being followed. It was impossible to tell if my suspicion was real or imagined. Aware that to the rest of the population it seemed as though I was on my own, I kept my head down and avoided making eye contact with anyone. It was a relief to round the final corner and see the welcoming red brick of the Dearly D in front of us.

'Wow. That's some crowd,' Owen observed, tearing his gaze away from a sporty Polo GTI to eye the mixture of living and ghosts on the pavement outside. 'Is it always this busy?'

'Most of the time,' I replied. 'We're the best in town and word travels fast, even amongst the dead.'

Owen frowned. 'Isn't that sign rubbing it in a bit?'

I followed his gaze. The D from Dearly had dropped off, making it *The Church of the early Departed*. 'They should probably get that fixed,' I agreed, grinning. 'Don't take it personally.'

We joined the queue and filtered into the church. Regulars nodded to me and gave Owen an appraising once over. He didn't say anything but I knew he wasn't comfortable and I made a note to introduce him to a few of the less eccentric ghosts after the service. The sooner he made friends and realised he had nothing to be scared of, the better.

Celestine spotted us as soon as we got past the double doors at the back. She was standing near the pulpit, chatting to Minister Guthrie. Smiling, she patted his arm and came towards us as we threaded our way down the aisle.

'You must be Owen,' she said, after greeting me. 'I've heard a lot about you.'

I cringed, hoping she wasn't going to mention the incident with Jeremy in my room. Owen gave a nervous cough. 'Nice to meet you, Miss Thackery.'

My aunt laughed. 'Call me Celestine. There's no need to look so worried. I don't bite, in spite of what Skye has probably told you. Why don't you take a seat?

The service will be starting soon.'

Scanning the pews, I searched for a friendly face to babysit Owen. My eyes came to rest on Alex, a seventeen-year-old ghost who'd been coming to the Dearly D for a few months. He'd been struck by lightning on Primrose Hill almost a year ago and we hadn't worked out why he hadn't passed across yet. He was pretty contented with his ghostly existence, however, and I reckoned he'd be a calming influence on Owen. 'Come on. Let me introduce you to Alex. He'll look after you while I'm working.'

The service was one of the busiest I'd seen for a long time, with plenty of spirit action. Every pew seemed full and it was standing room only at the back. Even if I squinted, I could barely make out the faces of the shadowy figures that hovered there. One of the living in particular stood out. He was dressed from head to foot in black and my gaze strayed to him several times, for reasons I didn't understand. I thought I'd seen him before but with so many regulars it was hard to be sure. Owen claimed my attention more, though, and I couldn't help watching him with anxious eyes. He seemed to be interested in what was going on but I was dreading his reaction if a ghost passed across. Would he be reminded that his future was the same or had my earlier reassurances soothed his worries?

Thankfully, we reached Minister Guthrie's final

blessing without incident. There'd been the usual exchange of messages between the living and the dead; I'd even passed on a few myself. And Gawjus George had flashed Mrs Lavender an eyeful of his greying underpants in an attempt to get her attention, but she'd shooed him away with an annoyed wave of her hand and the service had continued. I'd noticed Isobel chatting to Tony with no sign that his sequinned suit bothered her and filed it away under 'Good News' to report back to Jeremy. I was even more pleased to see Alex and Owen laughing together and headed over to find out what the joke was.

'It's not so bad once you get used to it,' Alex was saying as I approached. 'You can go wherever you like and some of the other ghosts are a good laugh. It makes me wonder who was watching me before I died, though. If I'd known ghosts were everywhere, I'd never have felt the same about taking a slash.'

'No ghost would choose to hang around a toilet, Alex,' I told him. 'I mean, seriously, why would you go in there if you didn't need to – er – go?'

'Fair point,' he conceded. He held out a fist towards Owen. 'I'm off. Good chatting to you, man.'

Owen touched his own fist to Alex's. 'Yeah, you too.'

I waved Alex off and then turned to Owen. 'So? What did you think?'

'It takes a bit of getting used to,' he said in a thoughtful tone. 'And I felt bad when your aunt was passing messages between that woman who'd died of cancer and her mum, like it was something private and I shouldn't have been listening.'

I knew exactly what he meant. It was common for members of the congregation to get very emotional as the service went on and even the hardest souls cracked sometimes, especially when the death had been sudden or tragic.

'Sometimes we do private meetings, if the ghost or their loved ones can't face speaking in front of everyone,' I explained. 'But most of the people who come here have lost someone close to them and they try to help as much as possible. It's a bit like having an enormous step-family in some ways.'

Owen brooded for a moment. 'Do you think the cancer lady has long left?'

'Before she passes across, you mean?'

He nodded and I caught the shadow of sadness on his face.

'No,' I said, with a gentle smile. 'I think she's almost said everything she needs to. Then she can move on and rest.'

'And what about how her mum feels? Won't it be like losing her daughter all over again?'

His eyes were anxious and I knew he was thinking about passing across himself. The problem was, I didn't know how to reassure him. I'd never tried to help a ghost who wanted to hang around before. 'Most people seem happy when their loved one passes across,' I said, groping around for words that would help. 'It's like . . .'

Celestine appeared next to me. 'Think of it like this, Owen. Imagine someone you loved emigrated to the other side of the world. You'd want to hear from them, to know they'd got there safely, wouldn't you?'

Owen nodded. 'That's what Skype is for.'

'OK, so think of the Dearly D as Skype for dead people. They contact their family through us to tell them they're all right. Then they find they have to move on, to somewhere really remote where there's no phone signal, no computers and no postal service. But because they had the chance to tell their loved ones where they were going, the people they're leaving behind don't worry about them so much.'

He mulled over her words. 'Wouldn't it be better if they didn't go to the remote place? Why can't they stay here, where they can still talk to their family?'

Smiling, Celestine said, 'Some do.' She paused and her voice softened. 'But the people left behind start to forget. They don't call in so often and eventually stop coming altogether. It's not their fault; life gets in the way and they have to deal with it. All the ghost can do is watch as the people they love get further away.'

Owen stared at her wordlessly, his eyes glittering like pewter under the lights above us. More than anything, I wanted to reach out and hug him and realised for what felt like the zillionth time how impossible it was.

'I wouldn't wish that on anyone,' Celestine went on, holding his gaze. 'It hurts. Some ghosts get angry and take it out on their loved ones. Others spend their time following them around, desperately hoping for a sign that they still care. We do what we can but, like anything, the ghost has to want our help and needs to be ready to move on.'

'I don't want that to happen to me.' Owen's words were tight, as though he was struggling to get them out. I could hardly blame him; it couldn't be what he wanted to hear. 'This whole thing sucks.'

'I told you, there's no rush to pass across,' I said, trying to soothe him. 'Your family are devastated to lose you and you're still adjusting to being a ghost. Give it a while.'

'Skye is right,' Celestine said. 'There's plenty of time. But you might want to start thinking about what's holding you here so that, when the time is right, you know how to let go. Otherwise, I'm afraid you'll have a very painful future ahead of you.'

She smiled in sympathy, pressed her hand against my arm and turned away. Owen's eyes sought mine. 'My family are going to forget me, aren't they?'

I felt the tell-tale prickle of tears. 'No, they'll never forget you, that's not what she meant. But eventually, they will move on. They have to.'

His gaze shimmered and he blinked hard. 'But I'll always have you, right?'

For the first time, I truly understood what my aunt had been trying to tell me. There could be no future for me and Owen. He'd always be sixteen years old, for a start, while I got older every year. Sure, we'd figured out a way to snog but that would be as far as it ever went. We'd never get married or have children and, although those things weren't so important to me now, maybe they would be later. As much as I didn't want to face it, Celestine was right; a relationship with Owen would only bring me misery, no matter how hard we tried to make it work. I also knew that now was the worst possible time to tell him so.

I forced a weak grin. 'Of course. You're not getting rid of me that easily.'

He grinned back, relief etched all over his face. 'Damn.'

Right on cue, Celestine's voice rang out. 'Skye! I could do with some help.'

I pulled a rueful face. 'Sorry. Duty calls.'

'No problems. You've got stuff to do. I should get going, leave you to it.'

I threw him a concerned look. 'Why don't you stick around? I'll only be about half an hour. You could chat to some of the other ghosts.' Gawjus George caught me glancing around and waved two dirt-encrusted hands in my direction, with a toothy grin. 'Or not.'

Owen shook his head. 'Nah, I'm going to head off. I've got some thinking to do. Maybe I'll hitch a ride in a killer set of wheels.'

'OK,' I said, then hesitated. We were supposed to be going to the cinema at the weekend. Should I remind Owen, after everything that had happened tonight?

'So I'll see you on Saturday?' he asked. 'I can't wait to see the film.'

Which answered that question. 'Yeah. I'll drop by the lake in the afternoon.'

'OK,' he said, smiling. 'It's a date.'

He waved and turned to go. I watched him leave with a heavy heart, wishing he'd picked another word. The knowledge of what I had to do lay boulder-like in my stomach. The last thing our trip to the cinema could be was a date.

Chapter 11

In spite of some heavy hints from Megan, I ignored Nico's invitation to sit next to him on the coach to the Tower of London. I had no plans to get close enough to let him try a repeat of his previous behaviour, no matter how heavily Megan hinted. Let her think he was Mr Perfect; I knew different.

The Tower itself seemed busy for a Friday morning. I counted at least three other school trips next to the entrance, their teachers looking every bit as frazzled as ours, and there was already a queue of snap-happy tourists waiting to go inside.

'Split into your groups,' Miss Pointer called, once we'd passed through the ancient stone arch and were assembled at the bottom of Tower Green. 'You have two hours to complete these worksheets and collect evidence for your coursework on traitors. One worksheet per group and we'll meet here at midday for our group tour before lunch. We will be catching up with you around the Tower to make sure you work with the people I assigned you to.'

Was I imagining it or did Miss Pointer stare at me as she said that last bit? Bang went any idea I'd had of tagging along with Megan's group. Ellie threw me a contemptuous look and deliberately turned her back. Sighing, I rummaged in my bag for a pen. When I looked up, Nico was standing next to me.

'Ready?'

'I suppose so.'

Megan slid her mobile out of her pocket. 'Text me if you need any help. Otherwise, I'll see you at lunch.' She squinted up at Nico with mock fierceness. 'And don't try anything funny. She knows karate.'

I bit back a grin. The only karate I knew was from an old eighties film we'd watched a few weeks ago. Somehow, I didn't think the 'wax on, wax off' routine was going to scare Nico. But I wasn't too worried; like Celestine said, if he was going to try anything, it wouldn't be somewhere busy like the Tower, in spite of his suggestion that we'd be alone at some point. My only real worry was that I'd fall under his spell again and I only had to remember his chilling behaviour at Highgate Cemetery to avoid that.

'I'll be fine, Megan,' I said, smiling. 'Catch you later.'

'I'll protect her, don't worry.' Nico tried to place an arm around my shoulder. I smacked it away. Megan, on the other hand, practically swooned. Strike up another point for Nico, I thought darkly. At this rate, she'd be running his fan-club by the end of the day.

'So who's going to protect me from you?' I asked, as Megan and her group huddled together to decide where to go first, leaving the two of us alone.

Nico pointed at a pair of Yeomen Warders not far from where we stood. 'Look around. There's plenty of Beefeaters for you to call on.'

Curiosity got the better of me and I peered at the men in their distinctive navy blue and red uniform. They were certainly eye-catching, I'd give them that; I wouldn't have any trouble spotting one if I needed back-up.

'The first question is about famous prisoners,' I said, transferring my dubious gaze to the worksheet. 'Do you really think Miss Pointer will know if we spend the next couple of hours in the gift shop and Google the answers when we get home?'

Nico studied the map we'd been given. 'I think the cuddly Beefeater teddy bear you'd buy would give you away and there are only so many jars of Ye Olde English Honey I can stand seeing, so let's go.' He looked up from under his enviously long eyelashes. 'Unless you're really afraid?'

I stared at him, unable to make up my mind. On the

one hand, he'd scared me witless that night in February but, on the other, I remembered how close we'd once been; I'd thought we had something special and I had trusted him with my deepest secret – he was the only living person outside my family who knew I was psychic. Which one was the real Nico? 'I'm not scared of you.'

He must have read my uncertainty. 'Look, Skye, I know I've been an idiot and you have no reason to trust me but, for what it's worth, I'm sorry about what I did in the cemetery. I'd just got back from Romania and my head was all over the place.' His black gaze rested on me. 'I wanted to impress you, to make you see that I wasn't ordinary like the other kids in school. But I went about it the wrong way. I should never have tried to pressurise you the way I did. I'm sorry.'

I didn't know what to say. With those smouldering good looks and air of mystery, Nico was a million miles from being ordinary. But there was no getting away from the fact that he was involved with something bad and that something had changed him, made him dangerous. Some girls liked that in a boy but they didn't carry my secret; the last thing I should do was get involved with him again. So why was I having trouble keeping that at the forefront of my mind? 'You used me.'

He shook his head angrily. 'No. I told you before, I didn't ask you out because you could see ghosts. I had no idea about your gift until later. After my trip to Romania, it made sense to get you to help me.'

Troubled, I chewed my lip. 'How do I know you won't try it again?'

Nico went still. 'Things are different now. Don't ask me to explain because I can't.'

'Can't?' I echoed in derision. 'Or won't?'

His jaw clenched. 'It's complicated. You'll just have to trust me.'

'How can you expect me to trust you after everything that's happened?' I demanded, trying to ignore the battle I sensed was going on inside him. 'Trust is something you earn, Nico, and this secrecy thing you hide behind is getting old.'

'Right,' he said in a soft voice. 'Because you don't have any secrets, do you?'

I glanced away. 'That's not the point.'

'No, it isn't. Everyone has something they want to keep hidden from the rest of the world, for whatever reason. I told you all my secrets when we were together, although I'd be the first to admit I screwed things up big time.' He gripped my arms and forced me to look into his eyes. 'So it's not that I don't want to be honest with you. It's that I don't understand everything myself yet.'

As I stared up at him, I realised something was different. Not with the way he looked; he was still the same boy I'd known and loved but there was a subtle change in him I hadn't noticed before. I couldn't pin down what it was, though, and forced the thought away.

'What's not to understand, Nico? Your dad got you into some pretty evil stuff and you're following along blindly.' I shook his hands away. 'And don't try to convince me the Solomonarii are angels waiting to happen because I'm not buying it.'

With an impatient huff, he shook his head. 'Of course we're not. But it's not as black and white as you're making out. Being in the Solomonarii has . . . benefits.'

I opened my mouth and closed it again. If by benefits he meant being able to terrify the life out of me then he was right on the money. 'Like what?'

He hesitated. 'Let's just say I don't need your gift any more.'

Staring at him, I tried to work out what he meant. In the cemetery, he'd wanted me to help him control a ghost to pass some Solomonarii initiation rite. If he didn't need me to do that any more, it could only mean one thing; that he'd learned how to do it by himself. 'You passed the test,' I said in a flat voice.

'Yeah. I can do all kinds of things now. Controlling the weather was only the start.' He glanced around and his gaze settled on a pair of ravens hopping across the green. 'Watch.'

Frowning in concentration, he held out a hand to the birds and muttered something under his breath. The ravens cocked their heads towards him. One cawed harshly and shook out its feathers. Nico mumbled again but I still couldn't make out the words. The birds seemed to understand, though; the larger of the two flapped its wings and hopped clumsily across the grass. Then it leaped upwards and landed on Nico's outstretched arm. The other opened its beak and croaked again.

'I could make it do anything I wanted,' Nico said, lifting his hand and staring into its beady black eyes. 'The Warden here clips their wings so they can't escape, but it would try to fly over the wall if I told it to.'

A mixture of fear and revulsion ran through me. 'That would be cruel. Let it go.'

Nico shook his arm and spoke a single word. It sounded strange, like another language; Romanian, maybe? The raven spread its wings and jumped onto the ground. 'I didn't say I would,' he said, 'just that we understand each other. Like I said: benefits.'

Now that I came to think about it, hadn't he mentioned being able to communicate with animals before, that night in the cemetery? It was another talent of the Solomonarii and something else about them to make me uneasy. Controlling a single bird was one thing but what if he had a whole flock under his command? Or a pack of rats, or wild dogs? Suddenly my mind was awash with the horrible possibilities. Then I remembered the affinity I'd felt with him, even before I'd told him about my gift, and the truth dawned on me: in a lot of ways, Nico wasn't so different to me. We were both teenagers struggling to deal with being different, with a fate we hadn't really chosen. Maybe I was being too hard on him. I gave myself a mental shake and the gnashing teeth of the dogs faded away; clearly, I'd been watching way too many horror films. 'So what are you, Romania's answer to Dr Doolittle?'

His eyes glittered with amusement. 'If you like. I'm trying to show you that I don't need your help any more, so you can stop worrying that I'm only interested in your gift.'

If he was trying to make me feel better, it wasn't working. 'There's still the small matter of the ancient evil clan you belong to.'

'The Solomonarii aren't evil,' he insisted. 'OK, so they haven't always been saints and some of the things they do are questionable but maybe I can change that.'

Folding my arms, I scowled. 'That's not what you thought in the cemetery.'

He frowned and once again I caught a glimpse of some inner turmoil.

'I was an idiot then,' he said and let out a sigh. 'Like I said, it's complicated. But believe me, the last thing I want is for the Solomonarii to hurt anyone else.'

Anyone else? I stared up at him, trying to work out what he meant. According to Mary, the Solomonarii were a danger to the living and the dead but this was the first time I'd heard Nico acknowledge the fact and I wished once again that I knew more about them. Coupled with his cryptic comments about complications and things not being black and white, I was starting to wonder if something had happened to shatter Nico's rose-tinted view of the Solomonarii. More than anything, I wanted to believe that Nico could use the powers they had given him for good. The problem was that he'd lied to me before and I couldn't be sure this wasn't another ploy to suck me in. But as Celestine had once suggested, maybe somewhere underneath the new Nico lay the old one.

Exhaling slowly, I pushed the doubts aside and made up my mind. 'In the interests of getting this coursework out of the way, I'm giving you the benefit of the doubt,' I said, waving the worksheet in front of him like a shield. 'Don't go thinking I trust you, though, and don't try anything funny. Like Megan said, I know karate.'

Nico threw me a relieved grin and raised a questioning eyebrow. 'Yeah, about that. You do realise that using chopsticks doesn't automatically make you a black-belt, right?'

'Oh, I think you'd be surprised,' I replied, turning towards the nearest tower and flashing a sunny smile over my shoulder. 'It really all depends on where you stick them.'

* * *

The rooms where they'd kept the traitors imprisoned weren't exactly plush. In the past, they'd often been flooded with foul-smelling water from the nearby Thames and rats snatched whatever food was tossed to the unfortunate prisoners. I didn't want to think about how many must have died in that squalor before they reached the gallows. According to the interactive displays, one of the inmates had been an innkeeper accused of sorcery. Looking around, I was grateful the display wasn't one hundred per cent interactive; there was no sign of the so-called sorcerer himself, or any other of the ghosts reputed to haunt the towers. There were plenty of tourists, though; both Nico and I were glad when we'd answered the last question and could head out of the congested rooms to a gravel-strewn pathway around the back of the armouries.

Leaden clouds overhead were adding to my subdued mood. The buildings loomed over us, creating a threatening atmosphere. Hardly anyone had ventured around this side of the Tower; there wasn't much to see, apart from a pair of ravens pecking at the gravel. I'd read that ravens had always been at the Tower and it was rumoured that something terrible would happen if they left. Suddenly, I was glad Nico hadn't made them fly away; superstitions sometimes had an element of truth behind them.

Heading towards a nearby bench, I sat down. 'Come

on, let's go over the questions to make sure we didn't miss anything.'

Nico sprawled beside me, his long legs making mine look shorter than ever. 'Why do you care so much about doing well at school? It's not like you're going to need the qualifications in your kind of work.'

I stared at him. 'What's that supposed to mean?'

He shrugged. 'Aren't you going to work at the Dearly D with your aunt? I don't suppose they'll care about whether you've got a GCSE in media studies.'

I shifted uncomfortably. 'Maybe I want to be more than just a psychic.'

Nico threw me a measuring look. 'Why would you? People who can do maths are everywhere.' Lowering his voice, he leaned closer. 'People who can talk to the dead aren't. We're not like everyone else, Skye. We can do so much more. I didn't understand that until my father introduced me to the Solomonarii.'

He had a point, I supposed; I'd known all my life that I was different. But that didn't mean I couldn't do a normal job, did it? 'What do you mean, "We can do so much more"? Like what?'

'Ghosts are the spirits of people who've died but who aren't ready to pass across, right?' When I gave a slow nod, he went on. 'You spend all your time trying to find a way to get them to the astral plane, even though they don't always want to go. So why not let them stay?'

I opened my mouth to reply and closed it again. There were a hundred reasons why ghosts needed to pass across and, if he'd asked me a few weeks ago, I'd have happily reeled them off. But that was before I'd met Owen, with his desperation to stick around, and now I wasn't so sure that moving ghosts on was always the right thing to do. No one had ever tried to get rid of Mary, that was for sure. Shouldn't ghosts have some kind of say in whether they passed across? 'But what would they do? Most of them can't figure out how to leave their haunting zone by themselves.'

Nico smiled. 'The Solomonarii have been working with ghosts for centuries. We take lost souls and provide them with tasks to do, give them a life and a purpose again. It's win-win.'

A memory stirred in my mind as I recalled something Mary had said when I'd asked her about the Solomonarii. I fired an accusing glare his way. 'Don't give me that, those ghosts are known as the Eaten, as in consumed. It doesn't sound like much of a partnership to me.'

Nico looked away. 'It's not perfect,' he admitted, a pensive expression crossing his face. 'We offer them a way to be bound to the earth forever, so that they never have to leave. And we listen to them. There's a price for all that.'

My thoughts strayed to Dr Bailey, the ghost at school. He'd spent the sixty odd years since his death bellowing ineffectually at the living students around him, trying to get them to obey him. Until I'd arrived, none of them ever had. How would he react if someone made him feel important again and offered him a way to make a difference? Would he turn it down, even if there was a cost attached? I didn't think so. Then something occurred to me. 'Wait. Can you actually see ghosts now?'

'Sort of,' he said. 'From what you've said I don't see them like you do. It's hard to explain, but imagine you were watching TV and it wasn't tuned in properly. You'd see flickering, shadowy figures and the voices would be distorted. That's what I pick up when there's a ghost around.'

I thought about that. If what he was saying was true then he could hardly have missed Dr Bailey. 'Have you met the school ghost?'

Nico frowned. 'Old bloke, big moustache, hangs around the entrance hall and shouts a lot. I try to keep out of his way.'

'Tell me about it.' I shuddered. 'The first time I met him he gave me lines.'

Nico pulled a face. 'You should definitely help him to move on.'

The thought had crossed my mind once or twice. Why was Dr Bailey still at the school? Maybe I'd try and find out when we got back but right now I had other things on my mind. 'What exactly does the Solomonarii get out of this partnership?'

'This and that,' Nico replied, his gaze flitting away evasively. 'I'm not one hundred per cent sure. Information, I suppose.'

He was being deliberately vague and I couldn't help thinking back to the troubled look I'd seen in his eyes earlier. But what he was saying kind of made sense; after all, information was currency for some people. Imagine if a businessman found out what products his competitors were developing, or if a poker player knew what cards his opponents held? They'd be able to outflank everyone and make big money. A darker thought occurred to me. What if a ghost could switch off a burglar alarm or memorise a safe combination? That was the kind of information which would be incredibly valuable to the criminal community. And I still didn't like the description 'Eaten', no matter how much Nico described it as an acceptable price for regaining something resembling a life. It didn't make it sound like much of the ghost survived the experience. 'I don't know —'

Nico sat up straight and cut me off. 'Look, I'm still learning about it myself. There's a lot I don't understand but they're not as evil as you make out. My dad wouldn't have got me involved with them if they were.'

His voice lost confidence as he mentioned his father, almost as though he was questioning his dad's motives himself, and again I wondered if something had happened. Or maybe my constant assertions that the

Solomonarii were monsters had taken effect. A snake of guilt slithered uncomfortably through me. I hadn't even met Mr Albescu and I'd already convicted him of being a terrible father. It was possible he didn't know what I knew about the clan's shady past. Then again, he couldn't be that innocent if he'd initiated Nico.

'Let's say you're right and what the Solomonarii do is distressing to the ghost. Maybe once I've learned more about what they do, I can make things better for them,' Nico went on, reaching for my hand and dipping his head to fix me with intense, pleading eyes. 'Don't judge me based on rumours and fairy tales, Skye.'

I gazed at him, confused. Part of me knew that I couldn't be wrong about the Solomonarii; everything about them made my sixth sense tingle with apprehension. But I couldn't help wondering if Nico had a point. And, as I sat there struggling with my conscience, another part of me was aware of his fingers entwined with my own, his face close enough for me to feel his breath tickling my cheek. My pulse began to quicken. If I leaned towards him now our mouths would meet, and suddenly there wasn't anything I wanted more. Gazing into Nico's eyes, I knew he felt the same.

The harsh caw of a raven next to my ear made me jump and pull away. Glancing around, I saw the bird perched on the back of the bench, its black eyes peering beadily between the two of us. It croaked again, as though in warning. Seconds later, Miss Pointer walked around the corner of the building and glared at us.

'I've been looking for you two. You're late for the guided tour.'

Gathering up my bag, I cleared my throat. 'Sorry. We were working hard and lost track of time.'

She threw me a disbelieving look. 'Then you'll be producing an excellent piece of coursework, won't you?'

Turning on her heel, she walked away. I went to follow but Nico caught my arm.

'See? There are some good things about the Solomonarii. We'd be in trouble if the raven hadn't warned us.'

The bird had saved me from more than just a telling off from Miss Pointer; I might have decided there was no future for me and Owen but that didn't mean I was free to go around snogging other boys. I gave a shaky laugh. 'Coincidence.'

Nico shook his head. 'Believe me, it wasn't. And in a few days, maybe I'll be able to prove that we're not all bad. Give me a chance, Skye.'

The words rang in my ears as I followed Miss Pointer to join the rest of the class. I'd given him a chance before and he'd hurt me more than I'd thought possible. Could I really risk letting him do the same again?

Chapter 12

It took around three seconds for Megan to figure out something had changed. By unspoken agreement, Nico and I left a respectable gap between us as we approached Tower Green and didn't look at each other. Megan wasn't fooled, though. She peered from my face to Nico's and back again, her eyes narrowing in suspicion. 'What happened?' she demanded. 'And don't say nothing because I can tell something did.'

I hesitated, wondering whether she'd make a puddle on the floor if I told her the truth. 'We talked.'

Megan's eyes widened. 'You snogged!'

I couldn't meet Nico's gaze. 'No, we didn't.'

A disappointed expression crossed her face. 'Well, you should have.'

'Megan . . .' I warned.

She tutted in an impatient fashion. 'You like him, he likes you – what's the problem?'

Fleetingly, I imagined what she'd do if I told her: laugh, probably, and tell me to stay off the drugs. 'There is no problem.'

'Good.' Megan turned to Nico. 'I don't know what you did to screw it up last time but make sure you fix it, OK?'

Nodding, Nico attempted a serious expression. 'I'm working on it.'

She folded her arms in satisfaction. 'Then my work here is done.'

As Miss Pointer rounded us up and herded us towards the waiting Beefeater for the tour, I snuck a look at Nico's profile and felt my stomach give a familiar lurch. I'd fancied him from the first moment I'd seen him and giving in to the attraction had always seemed like the most natural thing in the world. Now I realised those feelings had never really gone away and my flirtation with Owen had only reminded me what I was missing. I hoped Nico could make me believe I was wrong about the Solomonarii. I was in for heartbreak if he couldn't.

'How was the Tower?' Jeremy asked, when I trudged into the living room and sank onto the sofa. 'Did anyone lose their head?'

I wasn't in the mood for one of his jokes. 'You're not funny.'

He chuckled. 'I'm a little bit funny.'

I let out a leaden sigh. 'No, you're really not. The Pope is funnier than you.'

Mary drifted through the wall from the kitchen and eyed me with keen interest. 'I see thy wounded heart bleedeth again.'

My eyes narrowed. She might be able to read my aura but did she really have to treat my love life like it was a double-page spread in *Heat*? Folding my arms, I shook my head. 'I don't want to talk about it.'

'It may soothe thy soul to unburden thy sorrow,' she urged, a look of earnest sympathy on her face.

Oh for God's sake, it was like living with a cross between Oprah Winfrey and Mystic Meg. 'No, thanks.'

Jeremy looked around. 'Is Mary here? What is she saying?'

I rolled my eyes. 'She's channelling her inner agony aunt.'

Frowning, Jeremy peered at me. 'Is this about Owen?'

Why did everyone suddenly seem to think my business was their business? And why were all my problems the result of my supposed gift? Normal people didn't have to discuss their love life with the man fashion forgot and a witch old enough to be their great-great-great-great-great-great-great grandmother. 'No.'

Celestine came in from the kitchen, clutching a mug

of tea. 'What's going on? Did something happen with Nico?'

It was the last straw. 'Fine. Since you're all so interested, I talked to Nico. He explained why he acted so weirdly when he came back from Romania and told me a bit more about the Solomonarii.' Folding my arms, I glared round at them. 'They don't sound so bad to me. Nico said they actually try to help ghosts.'

Mary sucked in a ferocious breath. 'Wash thy mouth out with charcoal. The Solomonarii hath many a nefarious plot and seek thy help to see them through.'

I'd said it before and I'd say it again: sometimes she made about as much sense as Pingu. 'What kind of plot?'

Celestine stepped in. 'After you mentioned Nico the other day, I asked around again at the Dearly D. This time, they put me in touch with someone who claims to know a lot about the Solomonarii. His name is Gregor and I'm meeting him tomorrow afternoon.' She paused and studied me for a moment. 'I thought you might like to come along.'

Part of me welcomed the chance to find out more, but another part was afraid of what I'd learn. What if I discovered Nico had been lying when he'd claimed to want to change how the Solomonarii treated ghosts? 'What time?'

'One o'clock at the Dearly D.'

I chewed my lip. I'd promised Owen I'd pop by in the

afternoon before our trip to the cinema, and I was hoping to persuade him to let me talk to his sister. But Celestine was doing the face which meant she wasn't going to take no for an answer. I'd just have to hope this Gregor dude talked fast. 'All right, I'm in. As long as you promise to remember that Nico is trying to help.'

Mary huffed. 'He hath bound thine eyes with silken words.'

I sighed. 'Mary, I know you switch the TV on the moment we're all out. Get with the twenty-first century and speak English.'

Frowning in what seemed to be deep concentration, she gnawed on a blackened nail. Then she smiled. 'He talketh out of his arse.'

Celestine blinked and choked on her mouthful of tea. Even I smiled, in spite of the fact that she'd basically just called Nico a liar.

'Much better,' I said, nodding my encouragement. 'You're wrong but at least we're talking the same language.'

'We shall see,' she replied, watching Celestine mop up the mess she'd made. 'The leopard changeth not his stripes.'

'It's those stripy leopards you have to watch out for, definitely,' I agreed, hefting my bag onto my shoulder and heading for the stairs. 'If anyone needs me, I'll be in my room, contemplating the tragedy that is my life.'

The worst of it was, I decided as I dragged myself wearily up the stairs, I wasn't even joking; my life was tragic and my love life was practically non-existent. My whole life revolved around being psychic and it was getting me down. Suddenly, I missed my mum and the normality she brought with her. Being 'special' wasn't always what it was cracked up to be.

Saturday was one of those warm spring days when it's hard to believe anything could be wrong with the world. Even so, I had a heavy feeling in the pit of my stomach that no amount of birdsong could shift. Today, I'd find out more about the Solomonarii and maybe discover whether Nico really was talking 'out of his arse', as Mary had charmingly put it. I didn't know what I was more scared of: that he was lying to me or that the Solomonarii really were as evil as everyone else seemed to think.

By the time I got downstairs, my mood was filthier than an oil-slick and Jeremy's tuneless humming was doing nothing to fix it.

'What are you so cheerful about?' I muttered as I flicked the kettle on for a much-needed cup of tea.

He leaned against the kitchen counter. 'It's a nice day, I'm off work and your aunt tells me Isobel is getting along famously with someone at the Dearly D.'

My spirits lifted a little. 'Really? Is it Tony?'

Jeremy frowned. 'I can't remember his name but I

think he used to be in the police. Whoever he is, I owe him a pint. Isobel hasn't bothered me all week.'

Now that he mentioned it, I realised I hadn't seen her skulking in the trees outside for days. 'It's not Parking Pete, is it?' I asked dubiously, picturing the forty-something spirit who spent his days patrolling the King's Road in Chelsea, looking for cars with tickets about to expire and taking great delight in issuing a ghostly penalty notice when he found one. 'He was a traffic warden, not a policeman.'

'If he wears a uniform then he's your man,' Jeremy replied. 'Or Isobel's, with a bit of luck.'

I tried to imagine them as a couple and failed. 'She has the weirdest taste in men. First you, then Pete.'

His mouth quirked. 'Celestine doesn't seem to mind me.'

I glanced at the clock. 'Where is she, anyway? It's gone eleven and she didn't even try to turf me out of bed yet.'

'Shopping, I think. She muttered something about a shoe sale somewhere and said she'd be back at midday.' He nodded at the bubbling kettle. 'Milk, no sugar, thanks.'

Reaching for another mug, I dropped a tea-bag into it. 'Do you know anything about this Gregor?'

'Only what Celestine told me: that he's a native Romanian and very hard to get hold of.'

My eyebrows furrowed together. 'If he's so elusive, how come he's around exactly when we need him? That's a bit of a coincidence, isn't it?'

Pulling open the fridge, he delved inside and handed me the milk. 'Not really. Celestine tried to contact him when the thing with Nico first happened. It's taken this long for him to get in touch. He's a gypsy, I think, and spends most of his time travelling.'

I digested this new information as I handed him a mug of tea. The only travellers I'd ever seen were the ones who turned up for the Gypsy Brae festival in Edinburgh each summer and they'd been more interested in whisky spirits than any other kind. 'What makes him an expert on the Solomonarii?'

Jeremy blew on his drink and shrugged. 'I've got no idea. I don't even know if he's psychic, just that he's the man to talk to if you want to know about Romanian folklore.'

It was a deeply unsatisfying answer, I decided as I carried my tea back to my room to call my mum for a chat. Even the usually reliable Google drew a blank when I typed *Solomonarii* into the search field; all it came back with were *World of Warcraft* references which seemed to be written by fans and could be feverish imaginings for all I knew. Clearly, if I wanted the answers to the questions that tormented me I needed to talk to someone with first-hand experience of the cult. I hoped that person would be Gregor. Otherwise I'd find out the hard way whether Nico was telling me the truth.

Chapter 13

The Dearly D was almost empty when Celestine and I let ourselves in later that day. Over in one gloomy corner, I could just about make out Gawjus George and Handsome Eddie arguing over a game of chess. I half expected to see Isobel with Parking Pete, but there were no ghosts other than the chess grand masters and definitely no Gregor.

'Are you sure he's coming?' I whispered and my hissed syllables seemed louder in the quiet church than if I'd spoken normally. 'Maybe he's the kind of traveller who hates being inside a building.'

I'd built up quite a mental image of Gregor since my conversation with Jeremy earlier that day. He'd be a big man, with dark curls, a moustache and a gold earring. His clothes would be colourful and his thick accent would make him almost impossible to understand. Now that I came to think about it, he sounded more *Pirates of the Caribbean* than Romanian history expert but the picture was too firmly fixed in my mind to dislodge. So when a smartly dressed, clean-shaven man pushed open the door of the Dearly D, I didn't put two and two together at first.

'Can I help you, sir?' I called, getting to my feet and heading down the aisle towards him. 'The next service doesn't start until this evening.'

He didn't stop walking. 'My name is Dr Mirga. I am here to meet Miss Celestine Thackery.'

I hesitated. The words carried the barest trace of an accent and the suit he wore looked expensive. His dark hair was neatly slicked back and he carried a leather briefcase. All in all, he wasn't the rakish gypsy I'd been expecting.

'Welcome, Dr Mirga,' my aunt said and I realised she'd followed me. She held out a hand. 'I'm Celestine Thackery and this is my niece, Skye.'

Dr Mirga inclined his head as he shook first her hand, then mine. 'Charmed.'

'Come this way,' Celestine said. 'There's a room we can use to talk.'

I stepped aside to let him pass and watched him fire an appraising glance around the church. His eyes swept past the ghosts without the slightest flicker, suggesting he wasn't psychic. Filing the information away, I followed him to the front of the church and into one of the meeting rooms we kept for private consultations with the living and the dead.

Once we were as comfortable as we were ever going to be on the hard chairs, Celestine didn't waste any time. 'Thank you for agreeing to see us, Dr Mirga,' she began. 'I know you must be very busy with your lecturing duties.'

'It is my pleasure,' he answered. 'And please, call me Gregor.'

My aunt nodded and turned to me. 'Gregor is a lecturer in Romanian history at the University of Bucharest. He's currently touring the academic world, passing on his knowledge.'

I felt the start of a blush rising from under my T-shirt. Gregor might be of gypsy origins but he was highly educated, well dressed and clearly super intelligent. OK, so I'd got the black hair right and he did have a gold stud in his ear but I still felt ashamed of the way I'd imagined him. It really wasn't like me to judge people before I'd even met them, apart from Nico's father and there were all kinds of exceptional circumstances there. Clearing my throat, I willed the redness to subside. 'Hi. Does that mean you're an expert in Romanian folklore?'

Gregor tilted his head. 'It is part of my country's history, which means I have studied it. What is it you want to know of the Solomanarii?'

Taking a deep breath, I plunged straight in. 'How

much do you know about them?'

His dark eyes were calm on mine. 'Theirs is not a name I hear mentioned very often outside Romania. Why do you ask?'

I glanced at Celestine, wondering where to begin. 'I think a friend of mine might be mixed up with them,' I said, after a moment's thought. 'But no one can tell us anything about them, it's all smoke and rumours. I don't know what to believe.'

Gregor placed his briefcase on the ring-marked coffee table and opened it. 'Firstly, I must warn you that the Solomonarii are shrouded in darkness. They are a secret society who prize their concealment above all else. For your friend to have heard of them at all is a very bad sign.'

He reached into the briefcase and took out a drawing, which he handed to me. It showed a cliff-top castle, complete with soaring orange-roofed towers and forbidding grey walls. Above the castle were thunderous dark clouds. The surrounding land was covered by a mixture of fir trees and bare branches, reaching out like skeletal fingers to drag me in. Feeling myself sway forwards, I blinked and looked away. The sensation disappeared.

'These documents are photocopies of some within the university's private collection and are not commonly seen. I have them with me to compare with others I might discover on my tour,' Gregor said, apparently oblivious to the effect the picture had on me. 'The building you see is called the Scholomance, also known as the Devil's Academy. Its exact location is unknown, but legend says it is hidden somewhere in the Carpathian mountains. It was once home to Prince Vlad Tepes, son of Vlad Dracul. Both were terrible men who lived during a blood-thirsty time in Romania's past. Now we believe it is used as headquarters for the Solomonarii.'

I thought back to the night in Highgate with Nico. He'd mentioned the Devil's Academy, I was sure of it, but he hadn't called it the Scholomance. I wondered if I should tell Gregor and decided against it; there'd be plenty of time to share later.

Celestine took the picture from me and studied it. 'But who are they?'

'The story begins in the fifteenth century, during the rule of Vlad Dracul. You have heard of him, perhaps, as the inspiration behind the novel *Dracula*?' He paused and my aunt and I both nodded. 'It was actually his son, Vlad the Impaler, who the story is supposedly based on. The name Dracula translates as *Son of Dracul.* Since the word *dracul* can mean *devil*, you begin to see where the rumours of evil-doing have their roots.'

A sudden burst of rain rattled against the window, making Celestine and me jump in our seats. Uneasily, I glanced up at the darkening sky outside; what had happened to the warm spring weather I'd seen that morning? 'The Solomonarii aren't vampires. Nico told me that.'

A flicker of something showed in Gregor's eyes at the mention of Nico's name but he didn't pick up on it. 'We don't know what they are. Vlad Dracul was a knight of the Dragon Order, an ancient Christian sect who would go to any lengths to protect their native lands against invasion from the Turks. Perhaps his son used this noble order to further the deeds of the Solomonarii.'

The history lesson was beginning to grate on my nerves. 'What deeds?'

'They say there are nine members at any one time. Each must learn the crafts of the order and must pass a series of initiation rites before they are considered a full member. The crafts include controlling the weather, speaking the language of animals and controlling the dead.'

I thought back to the way Nico had manipulated the weather and spoken to the ravens. Celestine gripped my hand sympathetically, before asking, 'Who teaches them how to do these things?'

Gregor took out another drawing but didn't pass it across. Instead, he fixed us with a serious look. 'There is a tenth member, one who never leaves the Scholomance and is master of all the others. He is said to belong to the devil and teaches the rest their art. Vlad the Impaler was rumoured to be one such master and I expect there have been many more since his death. He commands their actions.'

Outside, the rain continued to batter at the window

and the wind howled around the building. Fleetingly, I remembered how the Solomonarii controlled the weather and wondered if one of them was nearby. Gregor seemed unfazed, though, and held out the sheet of paper. I hesitated, recalling the way the last image had affected me, then took it and showed it to Celestine. It was a rough drawing of a square talisman with nine symbols carved deep into it. I traced the marks with one finger. 'What does it do?'

He folded his hands in his lap. 'I cannot say. The original drawings came to the university decades ago and, despite many years of research, we are no closer to deciphering the symbols or locating the Scholomance. Perhaps it no longer exists.'

Thinking back to what Nico had told me about the Devil's Academy, I had a hunch it still existed. 'Isn't there a chance that you've misunderstood what the Solomonarii do? My friend told me they try to help the dead, not control them.'

'Ah yes, this friend. You mentioned his name earlier, Nico, wasn't it?' Reluctantly, I nodded. 'And he is of Romanian descent?'

Again, I tipped my head. 'He's not a bad person.'

Gregor smiled in a thin-lipped way. 'Perhaps not yet. But if he is truly involved with the Solomonarii, it is only a matter of time before he is corrupted.' He must have seen something in my face because his smile vanished.

'You do not think so? Let me explain what happens to a spirit the Solomonarii try to "help", as you call it. They start by luring the weak ones in with wild promises, of a physical existence again, say, or eternal life in this world. Blinded by these promises and its own desperation to live again, the spirit undergoes a ritual to become something more than merely a ghost. They become a creature neither living nor dead, who survives by drawing the life out of others. All sense of who they were before is lost and they exist in the shadows of this world, as insubstantial as ghosts but drawn to the living by an irresistible force. It is this that the Solomonarii use to control them.' He stared solemnly into our horrified faces. 'They become the Eaten.'

At the words, an almighty clap of thunder rumbled outside the window. A split second later there was a crash in the church and howls tore through the building. Heart racing, I leaped to my feet and yanked open the door. Wind tugged at my hair and clothes as I battled my way into the church, where George and Eddie were gazing towards the entrance doors with terrified expressions.

'It'sh the apocalypshe!' Eddie cried toothlessly, his bottom lip quivering millimetres away from his flaring nostrils. 'We're all doomed!'

'Actually, I think it's just the wind,' Celestine said in a more practical voice, hurrying forward to close the banging doors before they blew off their hinges. 'But extra points for atmospheric hysteria, Eddie.'

I wasn't so sure it wasn't one of the Solomonarii and a shiver ran down my spine. Eddie and George seemed reassured, though, and returned to their game of chess, darting grumbling glances towards both my aunt and the doors.

Gregor's voice in the sudden silence as my aunt finished wrestling with the doors made me jump. 'I must be going now. My presence here might put you in danger.' He was standing directly behind me, briefcase in hand. I hadn't heard him approach.

'How?' I asked.

He eyed me solemnly. 'I cannot be sure but this weather suggests one of the dark clan is nearby. Perhaps they seek to silence me again, as they have many times before.'

Celestine came towards us and said, 'Let's hope the bad weather is coincidental. Thank you for coming here and sharing your knowledge with us.'

He held out a rectangle of card. 'These are my contact details. We will need to talk again to work out how to proceed.' My aunt took the card and Gregor looked at me. 'Your friend may yet be saved but you should prepare yourself for the worst. The Solomonarii do not easily relinquish those they have claimed.'

An icy chill ran down my back. 'He really isn't bad,' I repeated, whispering.

A faint smile crossed Gregor's face. 'Then all is not lost.'

He shook our hands and began to walk towards the

back of the church. Then he stopped and directed a gimlet-eyed stare towards the ghosts. 'If you make that move, my friend, your opponent will have check-mate in another two. Choose wisely.'

George froze, chess piece held aloft, and gazed at Gregor, who winked and continued on his way. Seconds later, he was gone and the two ghosts were arguing furiously.

'I would have bet my best lip-gloss that he wasn't psychic,' I said, staring after him in dazed bemusement.

'Don't judge a book by its cover,' Celestine replied. 'Even professors have secrets and I get the feeling there's a lot more to Gregor than just history.'

I shook my head to clear it. 'Lesson learned, along with a lot of other things.' A feeling of disquiet overcame me as I mulled over everything Gregor had told us. 'Is that really true, about ghosts becoming kind of parasites?'

Celestine's expression was grim. 'I don't know. If it is, then it's too horrible to think about.' She paused and then spoke again in a rushed voice. 'You're not going to like this but I think you need to keep away from Nico, no matter how much he protests that the Solomonarii are a force for good.'

A few days ago, I would have agreed. But Nico had asked me to give him a chance to prove what he'd said was true and I intended to let him try. Celestine didn't need to know that, though. 'OK.'

My aunt blinked. 'That's it? No argument?'

'How can I argue after what Gregor told us? Besides, it sounds like he has more information to give us. I'd rather sit tight until we have all the facts.' I summoned up my most innocent expression. 'I think I left my Oyster card in the meeting room. I'll just go and check.'

If she was suspicious, she didn't show it but it was always a risk lying to Celestine; my aura tended to give me away. My Oyster was safely tucked in my pocket. What I really wanted to check was whether Gregor had left the photocopies he'd shown us behind. I wanted to show them to Nico, to see if he could add anything to the information Gregor had given us. It was a long shot, though, and I was fresh out of luck; the coffee table was empty. Clenching my fists in frustration, I turned in the doorway and bumped straight into Celestine.

'Find what you were looking for?' she asked in a soft voice, gazing directly over my head.

There was no point in lying. 'No,' I said, forcing a smile. 'It was here in my jeans the whole time.'

This time, she let her suspicion show. 'You do surprise me. Let's go.'

I didn't argue. The minute I got to the laptop I'd be logging on to Facebook. It was about time I extended a Friend Request of my own.

Chapter 14

It took all the courage I had to go to meet Owen at the lake. But I'm not the kind of person who avoids situations just because they're unpleasant, and knowing I had to break things off with Owen definitely qualified as unpleasant. After a minor interrogation about where I was going, Celestine agreed to drop me at Hyde Park. The freak thunderstorm had cleared but the wind hadn't and it bit through my thin jacket as I cut across the park. My top priority was persuading Owen to let me talk to his sister to see if I could work out what was holding him here. And then I planned to have the kind of heart-to-heart I'd never had with a ghost before. Actually, it was a conversation I'd never had with anyone before. What was I supposed to say? Somehow, 'It's not you, it's me' lacked the ring of truth. When the person you were dumping was a ghost, the problem really wasn't you.

My resolve stuck around for approximately three seconds once I saw him. He was standing in the middle of the lake, watching the boats circling round, surrounded by laughter and pleasure. Once again, I remembered that I was all he had and I knew I had to make him face up to his fear of passing across. He couldn't hang around this lake forever, growing lonely and bitter while I got old; I wouldn't let him.

He spotted me and raised an arm to wave. Moments later, he'd covered the water and was standing next to me.

'Hey,' he said, his flawed smile melting my worries away. He reached out a hand. 'How's my favourite psychic?'

'I'm OK,' I answered, lifting my index finger to meet his. There was a brief pressure on my fingertip and I felt a familiar thrill, then it was gone. 'How's my favourite ghost?'

'Feeling good, since you ask,' he said, his smile widening. 'Better than good, actually. I have something to tell you and I think you're going to like it.'

A little voice in my head whispered that I had things to tell him, too, but I refused to listen. 'Oh? Go on, then.'

He waved a finger at me. 'Uh-uh. This isn't the kind of good news you blurt out just anywhere. We need to find somewhere special.'

I raised my eyebrows. 'Did you have anywhere in mind?'

'Funny you should ask. Ever been on one of those open-topped bus tours of the city? You know, the ones which take in Buckingham Palace, Big Ben, Downing Street?'

'All the tourist traps, you mean?' I said dubiously and he nodded. 'No.'

He grinned. 'So let's do it. Be sightseers in our own town.'

I pulled out my purse and checked the contents. 'How much do you think it'll cost?'

'Depends if you count as a child or not,' he teased. 'I promise I won't makc you pay for me.'

'Thanks,' I said dryly. 'You're a real gentleman.'

Owen bowed. 'I do my best. Shall we go? If we leave it too long, we'll miss the film later.'

Here it was, my perfect opportunity to tell him the movie date was off. I opened my mouth to say it and then I saw his enthusiastic expression and the words died in my throat. 'We wouldn't want that, would we?'

His laughter rang out. 'You know, if I didn't know better, I'd say you weren't looking forward to this trip to the cinema. I guess action films aren't your thing.'

Forcing a smile, I laughed along with him. 'Not really.'

'But there've been some classics,' he objected. I barely listened as he began listing his favourite blockbusters of all time. Somehow in the next few hours, I'd have to bring the conversation round to his sister. And then the hard work would begin.

* * *

The tour bus was busier than I expected; London tourists were obviously a determined bunch, although they weren't a patch on the hardy sightseers we got in Edinburgh, where the rain could have your eye out if you weren't careful. We chose seats on the quieter top floor, away from a bunch of snap-happy Japanese visitors. They were far too engrossed in the commentary from their headphones to pay attention to a lone girl sitting at the back of the bus and that suited me fine. Apart from me and the tourists, there was only one other passenger: a dark-haired man who'd joined the bus shortly after Owen and me. He sat a few rows in front of us. Owen didn't give him a second glance but something about him nagged at me and, every now and then, my gaze came to rest on the uncut hair straggling down the back of his collar. I couldn't pin it down, whatever it was, and dismissed him from my mind. Instead, I huddled in my seat and tried to forget that my fingers had turned to icicles.

It took me until the London Eye to get Owen talking about his family. I sensed he was reluctant to discuss them and I wondered whether Celestine's words at the Dearly D had affected him more than I'd realised. Eventually, I spotted an opening when he mentioned a birthday trip on the Eye and I pounced.

'Did Cerys enjoy it?' I tried to keep my tone as casual as possible.

Owen snorted. 'Are you kidding? She's scared of heights and couldn't wait to get back down. At one point, a complete stranger even offered her a tenner to stop crying.'

I pictured the scene; Cerys sounded more high-maintenance than Mary. 'Did she take it?'

'No. I would have,' he said, shaking his head pityingly. 'Ten pounds is ten pounds, after all.'

'I bet she could be a bit of a pain,' I said, pulling a face. 'It makes me glad I'm an only child.'

As I'd hoped, Owen leaped to his sister's defence. 'She wasn't so bad. Sometimes, I actually quite liked her, even if she was drippier than a Cornetto in a heatwave.'

The bus turned onto Tower Bridge and I made a grab for the stainless steel railing as a gust of wind buffeted me sideways. Alarmed chatter broke out among the tourists but it didn't make them lower their cameras. Owen, of course, didn't so much as flinch.

'I'd still like to talk to her,' I ventured. 'About you, I mean. I think it might help.'

His grey eyes met mine. 'Her or me?'

'Both.'

He held my gaze for several long seconds, then looked away. 'We've been through this, Skye. It won't make any difference to how I feel about passing across.' He reached out and brushed my cheek. It felt like the caress of a moth wing. 'I want to stay here with you. Is that so hard to accept?'

I swallowed. 'Owen, you know that can't happen. You'll end up miserable. We both will.'

He sat in silence, gazing at the murky waters of the Thames as the tour made its way over the bridge towards the Tower of London. Unbidden, the memory of my visit there and my near-kiss with Nico sprang into my mind and guilt coursed through me. Was the real reason I wanted to help Owen to pass across so that I wouldn't feel so bad around him? Or was it really the best thing for him? It dawned on me that my motives were no longer as clear-cut as they had been.

'What if I told you that there was a way for me to stay?' Owen said, turning back to me. 'What if I met someone who could help me regain some of what I've lost?'

A chill ran down my spine which had nothing to do with the weather. I stared at him, trying to shake off the horrible suspicion crawling through my mind. 'What do you mean?'

'A man came to the lake yesterday evening. At first, I thought he was just watching the boats but eventually I realised he was staring at me.' A shadow of a smile tugged at Owen's lips. 'I spend the last few months thinking no one can see me and then I meet two psychics in as many weeks. Funny, isn't it?'

'Ha ha,' I agreed, my throat dry with anxiety. I hadn't told many people at the Dearly D about Owen, although they'd seen him on Thursday evening. What were the chances of a random psychic encounter, I wondered.

'The man told me his name was Ivan and he wanted to help me. He asked how I felt about being dead and then he said he had some friends who specialised in cases like mine, that they could help me become more than just a ghost.'

The white walls of the Tower loomed over the bus as we passed by. I shifted uncomfortably in my seat. 'Did he say how?'

Owen shook his head. 'No. But he did say that if they chose to help me, I'd be as good as alive again and I'd never have to pass across.' He fired an excited look my way. 'So? What do you think?'

My head was swirling in confusion and I didn't know what I thought. Before my meeting with Gregor, I'd have been doubtful enough but now I was deeply worried by the similarities between Owen's story and what I'd heard that afternoon. Who was this Ivan? Could he be a member of the Solomonarii? If so, was it a coincidence that he'd found Owen? There must be hundreds of ghosts around London. What had led him to mine?

'These friends,' I said slowly. 'Did they have a name?'

Owen jiggled impatiently beside me. 'What has that got to do with anything? Don't you understand what this means?' His eyes bored into mine and the flecks of amber danced. 'I'll be able to do all the things I miss, like racing my go-kart and running. No more half-felt touches and insubstantial brushing of lips, either. Once I get my substance back, I can kiss you the way I want to.'

He leaned towards me. Instinctively, I pulled away. His expression grew hurt as he sat back and studied me. 'You don't look as excited as I expected. What's wrong? Don't you want me to kiss you?'

Heart thudding in my chest, I took refuge in humour. 'It would look pretty weird if I puckered up on my own, don't you think?'

He tilted his head. 'True, but I think there's more to it than that.'

He was closer to the truth than he could possibly know, but I could hardly explain about my tidal feelings for Nico. Maybe I should tell Owen what I'd learned about the Solomonarii. Would he listen if I did? I'd have to be careful not to dump all the information on him at once but it was worth a shot. 'I'm worried about this man you've met. What he's offering you isn't natural. People die and sometimes they become ghosts. There isn't a way for them to come back to life, unless you believe in reincarnation and that's not what we're talking about here.'

The dark-haired man in front of us shifted in his seat. Owen ignored him and stared at me. 'I can't believe you're being like this. I thought you'd be happy.'

His face was a picture of confused resentment. Tears filled my eyes and I lowered my voice. 'I want what's best for you, Owen, and if that means losing you when you pass across, so be it. That's why it's so important for you to come and speak to Cerys with me. I think she's the reason you're still here.'

Confusion gave way to anger. 'Forget about passing across,' he spat. 'You've told me what happens to ghosts when they do that and it seems to me they just disappear. Admit it, you don't really know where they go once it's happened. They might fade away into nothing and you're making up a nice story to go with it so that you don't feel bad.'

The worst of it was that he could be right. Psychics believed there was an existence beyond this one but we had no evidence to support such an idea, in the same way that religions couldn't prove the existence of their afterlife. But I'd seen enough ghosts pass across to know that it was a pleasant experience and there was definitely life beyond what we understood by the word. Owen's fear went deeper than a fear of the unknown, though; he wasn't ready to let go of anything he'd once held dear and whatever I'd just told him I knew that Cerys wasn't the key to why he'd become a ghost. He simply wasn't prepared to give up on what his life had been. Until I persuaded him to give up his need to live again, he didn't stand a chance of moving on.

'Owen —' I began, reaching towards him.

He stood and stumbled backwards. 'Don't. You say

you want to help me but when I find a way to stay here, you don't like it.' Thrusting his hand into his jeans, he pulled out the pebble I'd given him. 'Well, maybe I don't need your kind of help. My way might be risky but it's not like I've got anything left to lose, is it?'

Holding his palm skywards, he tipped his hand sideways. The pebble rolled and fell. It hit the floor with a sharp clatter.

A ragged gasp escaped me. 'Pick it up, quick!'

His chin jutted upwards in defiance. 'Like I said, I'm going to do this my way. You'll see I was right eventually.'

As I watched, his edges became fuzzy, as though I was seeing him through frosted glass. Desperately, I bent down and clutched at the pebble. 'Take it!' I begged under my breath. 'Please, Owen, you don't know what's going to happen next.'

Out of the corner of my eye, I saw the tourists were whispering and pointing at me. I ignored them as a whining noise broke out around us. A hole was opening in the floor of the bus and I had no idea if anyone else could see it. Wide-eyed, I whispered to Owen, imploring him to take the stone. He peered down at the hole and clutched his head.

'What's happening? I feel like I'm going to faint.'

I lurched towards him, pointing at the pebble. 'You need this or you'll be dragged back to the lake.'

The whining increased. Groaning, Owen reached out

a blurry arm. His fingers clutched at the stone but it was too late. The noise reached breaking point and, with one final burst of high-pitched moaning, the hole sucked Owen downwards. I could only look on in horror as his fingers scrabbled at the floor ineffectually, then he was gone and the air was silent.

I sat staring at the space where he'd been seconds earlier, horror-struck. Then I lurched sideways and threw up down the side of the seat. As I sat up, wiping my mouth, I heard the single click of a camera. I looked up to see the Japanese tourists staring at me, their faces a mixture of confusion and interest.

'You OK?' one of them asked, in heavily accented English. A second lifted his camera to take another photo.

'Don't even think about it,' I growled, with all the menace I could muster. I guess he got the message because he lowered it again immediately and they all turned away, whispering amongst themselves.

Sinking back into my seat, I tried to make sense of what had just happened. My worry over Owen blinded me to the curious glances of the tourists. I'd heard of ghosts being pulled back to their haunting zones and knew it was every bit as horrible as it looked. And I had the added concern of wondering what Owen would do next with these new friends of his. I didn't doubt that he'd somehow been caught up by the Solomonarii; the coincidence was too great. The question was, would he listen to me long enough to convince him they were bad news?

It wasn't until we were about to get off, that I realised Owen wasn't the only passenger to have disappeared. The black-haired man who'd been sitting in front of us had gone, too. Frowning, I tried to remember when I'd last seen him. He'd been there as we crossed the bridge, because I'd seen him grab for support the same way I had. And I'd suspected him of eavesdropping at one point, too. Maybe he'd got off at one of the stops but I didn't remember seeing him go.

Shrugging off the thought, I headed for the underground. I needed to get to Hyde Park, to see if Owen was OK. Mary had warned me that the worst would happen if he lost the pebble and now I had to find out what that meant. If I was lucky, he'd be back at the lake, shaken but otherwise in one piece. Once I'd satisfied myself of that, I wanted to get home to the laptop. Apart from anything else, I had questions which needed answers. It was just possible Nico could give them to me.

Chapter 15

There was no sign of Owen at the lake. I spent a frantic hour searching for him, calling his name as though he was a lost puppy. When the sky started to darken, I gave up and headed wearily home.

I'd hoped to slip quietly upstairs when I pushed the front door closed behind me but my aunt had other plans. She'd posted Mary as a sentry at the top of the stairs, cutting off any chance of my sneaking onto the laptop to see if Nico had accepted my Friend Request.

Mary stood, arms folded, and stared down at me. 'Thine aunt seeks an audience with thee.'

I stopped four steps from the top. 'What about?'

She shrugged. 'Evil spreadeth a dark shadow ever further over the forces of good.'

I counted to ten under my breath. Who did she think

she was – Gandalf? 'Where is she?'

'Down the stairs, invoking the magical tablet,' Mary said, pointing a dramatic finger towards the living room.

Celestine was on her iPad when I found her. Jeremy had one eye on the snooker but hit the mute button as soon as he saw me.

'What's up?' I said, sitting down on the sofa and trying to look relaxed, even though I was burning to snatch the screen out of her hands and log onto Facebook.

She studied me intently. 'You tell me. I was going to suggest that we decide on a list of questions to email to Dr Mirga but it looks like you've got more important things to tell me.'

There was no point in lying, I realised; she'd suss me out before I'd finished the first sentence. Haltingly, I relayed the whole sorry tale. I saw Jeremy flinch when I described the way Owen had vanished and I wondered if he'd witnessed the same thing with another ghost. When I finished, Celestine looked very worried and even Mary was silent.

'Did you find him?' my aunt queried.

I shook my head. 'No. I think I'm probably the last person he wanted to see so he might have been hiding from me.'

Jeremy nodded. 'From what I've heard, it's a horrible experience but the ghost usually survives it intact. I don't suppose he'll have been feeling his best, though.'

It made sense that he'd be avoiding me if he felt rough, I realised. Maybe I'd go back tomorrow.

'Do you think the man Owen met is one of the Solomonarii?' Jeremy went on.

I spread my hands. 'How many other people go around offering once-in-an-afterlife opportunities to ghosts?'

He thought for a moment. 'Good point. In that case, how did they find him?'

I hesitated. 'I could always ask Nico.'

'No!' chorused my aunt, Mary and Jeremy all at the same time.

I blinked. 'Obviously I'm not going to come right out with it but I'm sure he doesn't know what he's got himself involved with. Maybe if I ask the right questions, I can find out exactly what the Solomonarii plan to do with Owen.'

Celestine chewed her lip. 'I don't know. Are you sure Nico isn't lying to you about how much he knows? He seemed pretty involved with them back in February.'

I couldn't argue but he'd seemed one hundred per cent genuine when we'd talked at the Tower. 'He told me he'd had a power rush when he first joined but now he can control things much better. He also said he wasn't interested in my gift any more, just – er – me.'

'I still don't know . . .' said Celestine.

Mary scowled ferociously. 'They be the Devil's

brethren and speaketh with forked tongues. Trust not a word which falleth from their lips.'

It wasn't the first time she'd spoken with such passion about the Solomonarii and it made me wonder if there was a story behind her venom. Had she known a ghost who became one of the Eaten? It couldn't be first-hand experience; there was plenty of spirit about Mary, no one would describe her as consumed. I opened my mouth to ask her about it, but the warning look Celestine sent my way changed my mind. Maybe I'd ask Mary about it when all this was over, but for now I was happy to bow to my aunt's better judgement.

'Even if they are as evil as you say, Nico isn't. He's still capable of making his own choices and he says he wants to help. I think he's being honest with me.'

Jeremy frowned. 'And if he's not?'

I didn't want to think about that possibility. 'I'd be surprised if he didn't expect me to research the Solomonarii after he told me about them. Maybe he even wanted me to.'

My aunt looked thoughtful. 'As a cry for help, you mean?'

Actually I'd meant in that boastful kind of way boys had, but her explanation was good, too. 'Yeah, that's what I meant.'

She nodded. 'You could be right. Maybe we should be viewing Nico as an innocent caught up in all this, although his behaviour so far doesn't make it easy.'

She was swaying towards having more faith in him and I realised I wanted her to think well of him. I needed more to tip the balance, a sweetener to seal the deal. 'There's something else,' I said in a slow voice. 'I got the impression that Nico was trying to find out more about what the Solomonarii actually do. He said something about wanting to change the way things were.'

'He's lied to you before, Skye,' Celestine said doubtfully. 'How do you know you can trust him now?'

'I don't know,' I said. 'Something feels different. At least let me talk to him about Owen. What harm can it do?'

Celestine stared deep into my eyes for a moment, and I wondered if she could see how close I was to falling for Nico all over again. Eventually, she nodded. 'But only about Owen. Don't mention anything about Gregor and what he told us, OK?'

'I promise,' I said, crossing my fingers inside the sleeves of my sweatshirt. 'Psychic's honour.'

She watched me all the way across the living room and I felt her gaze still boring into me as I mounted the stairs. She might have suspected how I felt but she hadn't said anything about it. That meant she trusted my judgement. I hoped she was right; where Nico was concerned, I wasn't entirely sure I could be trusted myself.

* * *

Nico still hadn't accepted my Friend Request and, by Sunday afternoon, I was ready to ask everyone I knew where he lived so I could go round and see him and I was cursing my stupidity in deleting his mobile number after we split up. Although I understood why he'd never taken me to his house when we were a couple, it was a real pain now. Megan was at a family party all day so I couldn't even pump her for details of her date with Charlie to pass the time. By way of a distraction, I took myself down to the Serpentine to check up on Owen but, if he was there, he wasn't showing himself to me. I had visions of him hovering around the island in the lake, keeping just out of sight. Eventually, I gave up and headed dispiritedly back to Highgate.

By the time I'd spent a sleepless night watching the hours crawl by and I'd dragged my sorry self into school on Monday morning, I was more on edge than an X Factor auditionee. Only Megan's smiling face when I met her for registration made me feel better.

'So?' I demanded when she didn't dish the dirt immediately. 'Tell me about the date of the decade. Did he hog the Häagen-Dazs or snog you over a Slush Puppy?'

She beamed shyly. 'It was Ben and Jerry's and we shared the Cookie Dough love.'

I grinned. 'Go, you two. When are you doing it again?'

'On Thursday. We're going ice-skating. Want to come?'

The last time I'd been skating it had been with Dontay and I'd woken up the next day covered in bruises. It wasn't an experience I was in a hurry to repeat, especially not as a gooseberry. 'I think I'm working.'

Her eyes twinkled. 'There are three whole days between now and Thursday. Anything might happen.'

I guessed she meant with Nico but I didn't answer her. By the time I'd tackled him about Owen, things were likely to be frosty enough between me and Nico. We wouldn't need a trip to the ice rink to chill our relationship any more.

I knew there was something going on with Nico long before I saw him outside our history class. I'd caught his whispered name too many times as Megan and I made our way along the corridors, and several kids I knew looked at me oddly as I passed them. Uncomfortably, I thought back to our trip to the Tower. Gossip spread faster than flu in our school; maybe someone had spotted us talking and started a rumour we were back together.

It wasn't until we reached the classroom that the real reason he was such a hot topic became obvious. He was standing at the back of the line, leaning against the wall. The left side of his face was covered in an ugly purple-black bruise and his eye was swollen and bloodshot. My mouth dropped open and it was clear I wasn't the only one who was shocked. Some of the boys were staring in open admiration, others avoided looking at him and the girls were conducting hushed conversations behind their hands as they darted curious glances his way. His gaze met mine for a brief second. Then he looked away, a stark warning not to ask him about it. Feeling as though someone had punched me in the stomach, I joined the back of the queue and tried not to stare.

'Oh my God, what happened?' Megan whispered. Her voice was barely audible but I knew Nico must know we were talking about him.

Shock numbed my thought processes. 'I don't know.'

Miss Pointer bustled up and unlocked the classroom. As we filed in, I thought Nico moved awkwardly and I wondered if he had other injuries. However he'd got them, it must have been bad.

He didn't speak as we settled into our seats. His uncharacteristic silence worried me even more; after Friday, I'd thought he'd at least have said hello and I didn't want to prod him in the back in case I hit another bruise. But neither could I survive the whole lesson without checking he was OK.

'Nico, are you all right?' I said in an undertone, leaning forward and pretending to rummage in my bag. 'What happened to you?'

His shoulders stiffened and he turned slightly in his seat. 'Leave it, Skye.'

Catching a glimpse of his bruised cheek and puffy eye,

I felt another wave of shocked concern.

'Did you get into a fight?'

'I said, leave it.' This time, the words had an undertone of anger and, as worried as I was, I knew it was pointless to keep asking. But his raised voice had caught Miss Pointer's attention. She glanced over at us and I saw her eyes widen as she took in Nico's face. Her gaze lingered for several seconds and I guessed she was debating whether or not to mention it.

'That's a nasty black eye you've got there, Nico,' she called. 'How did that happen?'

For a moment, I thought he wouldn't answer. Then he said, 'Playing rugby, miss.'

A ragged cheer went up from the boys. Miss Pointer raised her eyebrows. 'It must have been some match to cause so much bruising. Have you seen a doctor?'

Nico shrugged. 'It looks worse than it is.'

The teacher studied him. 'I doubt that but if it gives you any trouble, go and see the school nurse.' A faint smile crossed her face. 'I hope you won?'

He didn't return the smile. 'No. I lost.'

As Miss Pointer turned her attention to the rest of the class and the lesson got underway, Megan leaned towards me. 'I didn't know he played rugby.'

'He doesn't,' I replied, gazing at the back of Nico's head in grim bewilderment. 'So the question is, what was he really playing at to get so badly hurt?'

It must have something to do with the Solomonarii, I decided, but there were other questions I needed answers to more. If Nico, with all his powers, had come off worst, what exactly did he lose? And to whom?

One thing I was sure of: whether he liked it or not, Nico and I needed to talk. And this time, I wasn't settling for anything less than the full story. I wanted to know exactly what had happened to him and what he knew about Owen. Nico owed me the truth.

Chapter 16

I cornered him as we left the classroom. One look at my determined face and he agreed to meet me in the memorial garden at lunchtime. I half thought Megan would ditch her athletics practice to come with me, but she settled for making me promise to fill her in afterwards. If my suspicions were right, she wouldn't be getting the truth.

Nico was waiting on a bench in the quadrant which housed the memorial garden enclosure, when I walked in. My stomach somersaulted at the sight of him, but it wasn't only the usual surge of attraction I felt – the awkward way he was sitting filled me with anxious pity and I knew he'd been lying when he'd told Miss Pointer the bruises looked worse than they felt. More than anything, I wanted to wrap my arms around him.

'Hey,' I said in a soft voice as I approached. 'How are you doing?'

A flicker of pain crossed his face. 'I've been better.'

I felt a pang of guilt. The memorial garden benches were wooden, probably not the most comfortable seats when you were injured. Usually, I avoided this part of school, with its small bronze plaques to students who'd died too young, but I'd chosen it today because it tended to be deserted.

'Is there anyone else in here?' I asked, peering behind the bamboo canes in the corner with suspicion. The last thing I needed was for someone to eavesdrop on what was likely to be a difficult conversation.

'Doctor Bailey wandered through just now but he was muttering about queues in the canteen.' Nico shifted on the bench and gave a humourless smile. 'It's just you and me.'

'Good. Then you can tell me how you got hurt,' I said, perching on the bench beside him. 'And don't give me that rugby rubbish. You don't even play.'

For a moment, I thought he wouldn't answer. 'Would you believe I walked into a door?'

'No.' I gazed at him and hesitated. 'Were you doing something for the Solomonarii?'

He stared at the gurgling water feature, avoiding my eyes. 'Not exactly.'

'Then what happened?' I reached out a sympathetic

hand to touch his bruised cheek. 'Because if you don't mind me saying this, you look like hell.'

Nico slumped on the bench. 'I stuck my nose into something I shouldn't have, that's all,' he said and a trace of bitterness crept into his voice. 'The beating was to teach me not to do it again.'

I stared at him in horror. 'Who did this to you?'

He closed his eyes. 'My father. I waited until he was out and snuck into his study, trying to find out more about the ritual of the Eaten. I thought if I knew more about it, I could figure out a way to make it better for the ghosts.' His good eye opened and fixed bleakly on me. 'He came back before I was finished.'

Words failed me. I'd known the Solomonarii were dangerous but I hadn't expected they would turn on one of their own. Worse still, Nico's punishment had been delivered by his father. Any shred of doubt I'd had about whether Mr Albescu was unaware of his clan's murky past evaporated. 'Nico —'

He held up a hand. 'Don't tell me I should report him to the police. It was my own fault. If I hadn't been in his study, it wouldn't have happened.'

I gripped his hands. 'Listen to me, Nico. This is not your fault. Even if you were doing something you shouldn't have been, there's no excuse for hitting you. Has he done this before?'

'No. I've never actually seen him so angry.' He shook

his head, wincing. 'Believe it or not, I think it could have been worse.'

I supposed he was right, but what I was struggling to believe was how Nico was making excuses for someone who had beaten him black and blue. 'Once is enough. I know you don't want to but you should tell someone about this.'

'And then what?' Nico said, pulling his hands out of mine. 'I get taken into care? No one in their right mind would choose that.'

'You can't stay with him,' I insisted. 'Look at what he's done to you. Isn't there anyone else you can stay with – family or something?'

'The Solomonarii are all the family I have, Skye,' he replied in a flat voice. 'My mother's sister lives in London but she's always refused to have anything to do with my father and perhaps now I know why. Anyway, I can't leave. Not after what I found out.'

The breath caught in my throat. 'What do you mean?'

His gaze became stony. 'You were right about what the ritual does to the ghost. They use binding spells to keep the ghost inside a pentagram until the ritual consumes them. The images and descriptions in the books I found were horrific. I almost threw up at one point.' He brushed a hand over his face. 'I can't fool myself any more. There's no way what they do helps ghosts.'

'So get out while you can,' I urged. 'Track down your mum's family.'

He sighed impatiently. 'I told you, I can't. They've got something planned. After my dad had stopped hitting me, he rang someone. I suppose he thought I was unconscious but I heard him talking about the next ritual.' His gaze met mine. 'They've got a ghost lined up. It's going to happen tonight.'

My blood ran cold. 'Who is it?'

'I didn't catch his name. But my dad said he'd found him in Hyde Park. He told whoever it was on the phone that the ghost was desperate to live again and would do anything the Solomonarii told him to.'

I let my eyelids drift shut. 'He's called Owen.' I whispered.

Nico froze. 'You know him?'

Tears welled up behind my eyes. 'He's my – friend. He told me he'd met someone who was going to help him live again. I thought it must be one of the Solomonarii.' I hesitated. 'Owen mentioned a man called Ivan. He's your dad, isn't he?'

Nico groaned. 'Yes.'

Another thought occurred to me. 'What does he look like?'

'Like an older version of me,' he said. 'Tall, black hair, a bit grey at the temples. Less bruised, obviously.'

An image of the dark-haired man from the tour bus

flew into my mind. 'I think I've seen him. How much have you told him about me?'

Nico went pale. 'Everything. I thought you'd see we weren't so bad eventually and we could work together.' He let out a hollow laugh. 'How wrong was I?'

'So he found Owen through me.' As I spoke, Gregor's vivid description of how a ghost became Eaten loomed large in my mind.

He stared back at me and I could almost see the turmoil seething inside him. Sucking in a calming breath, I forced my heightened emotions to settle down. 'What are we going to do?'

Silence hung between us. Then he sighed and looked away. 'I don't know. I mean, I guess I've known for a while something wasn't quite right but I didn't want to find out for sure.' His dark eyes sought mine and I almost gasped at the misery I saw there. 'Dad's always been strange. Even when I was tiny, I knew he wasn't like other fathers, but I thought it was his sadness at losing my mum. Now I wonder if he mistreated her.'

I didn't know what to say. He'd never told me how his mother had died but I was starting to suspect it hadn't been from natural causes. How would I sleep knowing Nico was in the same house as the person who'd beaten him without a second thought? More importantly, how would he? 'Come and stay with us,' I said on impulse. 'I'm sure my aunt won't mind once I explain.'

Nico shook his head. 'He'd find me. Besides, if I stay, I'll be more useful. Maybe I can help your friend.'

I bit my lip. 'It's too dangerous.'

'It's riskier to leave. Then he'll worry who I'm telling his secrets to.'

I could see what he was getting at but I hated the thought of him being in danger. 'At least promise you'll try to find out where your mum's family are.'

Nico threw me a tired look. 'OK.'

Leaning towards him, I planted a soft kiss on his unbruised cheek. 'Thank you for trusting me with all this. It can't have been easy.'

He smiled. 'Are you kidding? Knowing I could confide in you was the only thing which made me come in today.'

I tilted my face towards him. 'I'm glad you did.'

Just as I was wondering whether it would hurt to kiss him again, the bell rang, making both of us jump.

'We'd better go,' I said reluctantly, getting to my feet. 'You will text me, won't you? Promise me you won't try to do everything on your own.'

For a moment, I thought he might refuse my request. Then he nodded. 'Keep your phone on. I'll text you once I know where we're meeting Owen.' He bent down and kissed me swiftly on the lips. 'When this is over, I'm going to do that properly.'

Try as I might, I couldn't stop the flutter of butterflies his words aroused. In spite of the circumstances, I was looking forward to that kiss. And now I knew that, previously, he'd had no idea what the Solomonarii were truly like, I could forgive him for being sucked in. After all, if my mum or Celestine asked me to do something, I didn't often question why, so it was only natural Nico would be the same with his father. And now that the truth was out, I couldn't deny something else any longer: Nico was well and truly back in my life.

Chapter 17

The moment I was clear of the crowds after school, I dialled Celestine's number.

'Come straight home,' she instructed as soon as I'd explained what Nico had told me. 'I'll see if I can contact Gregor. And, Skye? Don't take any shortcuts down secluded paths.'

I didn't argue. Having seen what Ivan Albescu had done to his own son, I dreaded to think how he might treat anyone else who got in his way.

Mary met me at the front door, a mournful expression on her grimy face.

'The time of reckoning approacheth,' she intoned as I swung the door closed. 'Blood will spill.'

'Let's not get carried away, Mary,' Celestine said, appearing in the hallway and pulling a face. 'We don't even know much about what's happening until Nico texts Skye.'

She turned and waved a warning finger. 'Evil hath woken and darkness lieth ahead. I feel it in my water.'

I turned to Celestine. 'Have you spoken to Gregor yet?'

She shook her head. 'No. Have you heard from Nico?'

I glanced at my phone. The text message symbol was noticeably absent from the screen. 'Maybe I should go to Hyde Park, to see if Owen is there and stop him from this madness,' I fretted. 'Or try to find his family and persuade them to help. I should have seen this coming and done more to get them involved.'

'Don't blame yourself,' Celestine said trying to soothe me. 'There's no way you could have known this would happen.'

I'd wondered about that all the way home. Was it a coincidence that Nico's dad had offered to help Owen or had he been chosen because of me? I thought back to the black-clothed man I'd seen lurking at the Dearly D; it had to have been Ivan Albescu. Maybe he'd spotted Owen with me and followed him back to Hyde Park. Or perhaps he'd selected him at random from all the ghosts there that evening. Whatever the reasoning, it was deeply unsettling; how many other ghosts at the Dearly D were in danger?

Jeremy poked his head into the hallway, his hand over the mouthpiece of Celestine's phone. 'It's Gregor.'

My aunt took the handset. 'Come on, Skye. He might

need to ask you some questions.'

A stab of anxiety cut through me as I dropped my bag and trooped through to the living room. What if Gregor said there was nothing we could do?

Celestine waited until I was sitting on the sofa next to her before setting her mobile to speakerphone and holding it between us. In terse sentences, she explained the situation to Gregor.

'This is very serious,' Gregor's voice crackled through the speaker once she'd finished. 'If the ritual completes, this ghost will be lost to you forever. At all costs, you must prevent the Solomonarii from completing the incantation.'

'Do you know what it actually involves?' Celestine asked. 'I expect there'll be some kind of binding spell but what else?'

'No one has witnessed the ritual and spoken about it but this much I can tell you. There will be a reversed pentagram inside a circle. Your ghost friend will stand within it. Each point of the pentagram will bear a candle to represent the element of fire. Water, earth and air will be symbolised as well. Most likely, the Solomonarii will have a knife for the ritual. You should take black pepper and salt if you are to have any hope of disrupting the spell.'

I blinked. 'Salt and pepper? Nico's father will be packing a blade and we're taking condiments to stop him?'

Gregor sounded unruffled. 'When the ritual is almost complete, throw them into the pentagram. This will break the spell and set your friend free.'

'Why can't we stop it before then?' I asked. 'Wouldn't it be safer for everyone?'

'If you act too early, the spell will not be affected,' Gregor explained. 'The safest thing would be to convince the ghost to stay away, but from what you have said, this seems unlikely.'

He could say that again. I couldn't even find Owen, let alone convince him to give up his crazy plan.

Celestine shifted uneasily on the sofa beside me. 'How will we know when the moment is right?'

There was a pause. 'You will know. The spirit will change, start to become what the ritual dictates. It is then that you must act. But perhaps I should come with you. I was due to leave London tonight but my appointments can wait.'

'I'd feel much better if you were there,' my aunt admitted and squeezed my hand. 'If what happened to Nico is anything to go by, the Solomonarii are more dangerous than we realised.'

'Owen is going to be OK, isn't he?' I asked, doubt creeping into my mind. 'Afterwards, I mean.'

Gregor cleared his throat. 'I do not know. This has never been attempted before, to my knowledge.'

My eyes met Celestine's. 'So it might not work at all.'

'Possibly not,' Gregor said. 'But it is your only hope if you wish to save your friend. I am at your disposal, should you need me.'

Celestine thanked him and, with promises to let him know if we heard anything from Nico, she hung up.

'I have a bad feeling about this,' Jeremy said, perched on the back of the sofa. 'Can't we call the police or something?'

Now there was a conversation I wouldn't mind overhearing. 'What would you say? "Yes, officer, I'd like to report some illegal incense use"?'

'Black magic isn't considered a crime unless someone gets hurt or pays a lot of money for it,' Celestine explained. 'The police wouldn't be interested in Nico's dad unless Nico wanted to press assault charges and, even if they were, there'd be nothing to stop him performing the ritual another time.'

I hesitated, wondering whether I should confess how I felt about Nico. 'There's something else I should tell you. Nico and me are kind of back together.'

Closing my eyes, I waited for the objections. When none came, I peeled back my eyelids and squinted at them.

'Well, duh,' Jeremy said. 'It was obvious something had happened and it didn't take a genius to work out what.'

'It is written all over thy face,' Mary agreed and then glared at me. 'Thou art a strumpet of the worst kind but mayhap thy love hath tamed the demon's heart.'

Which left only Celestine to comment. I held my breath.

'I suppose it's an improvement on kissing ghosts,' she said in a grudging tone and the breath whooshed out of me in a rush. 'Just be careful. He broke your heart before and he can do it again.'

I nodded. 'I will be.'

My phone vibrated in my pocket, making me jump. I tugged it out and opened the waiting text message. 'It's from Nico,' I said, swallowing. 'He says to come to the old keeper's cottage in Highgate Woods at midnight.'

Jeremy frowned. 'I don't remember seeing an old keeper's cottage in the woods. I thought they were all in use.'

My aunt looked thoughtful. 'There's a derelict house on the north side, I guess he means that. Does he say anything else?'

I glanced at the message again. 'No.'

'Then we have no idea how many will be there.' She threw me a rueful look. 'I suppose there's no point in trying to persuade you to stay here?'

'Absolutely none.'

Celestine nodded at Jeremy and Mary. 'Then it'll be five of us versus however many they bring. I don't think we can rely on Nico, it might be too hard for him to help.' Her face tense, she got to her feet. 'I'll raid the kitchen cupboards and contact Gregor. Then I suggest we get some rest. It's going to be a long night.'

Chapter 18

If you're the kind of person who believes in signs and portents, you'd probably have thought the weather was against us as we left at eleven-thirty to meet Gregor at the woods. The rain had started around ten o'clock and hadn't stopped since. To make matters worse, a fierce wind had sprung up which buffeted Jeremy's little Micra as we headed north to Muswell Hill Road and drove the rain into our faces once we'd arrived. I found it hard to breathe and it wasn't only the weather to blame. My anxiety for Nico and Owen was reaching new heights. Could we really save Owen with the meagre weapon we had, and what would it cost Nico if we did?

Gregor was waiting at Lodge Gate, dressed from head to toe in black. He nodded at each of us, including Mary. 'The gate is locked. We will need to find a place to cross the fence if we are to proceed.'

Jeremy looked up and down the road, squinting in the rain. 'We should split up. I'll stick with Skye if you go with Gregor, Celestine?'

My aunt nodded her agreement. 'Try to find somewhere away from the road. We don't want to get caught before we begin.'

Mary slipped through the iron gates and faced us from the inside. 'Mayhap the villains hath left a sentry. I will scent him out if so and meet thee here anon.'

She turned and melted into the woods, her faint glow soon eaten up by the darkness. Jeremy flashed his torch at me briefly. 'Ready?'

'As I'll ever be.'

Celestine patted my arm. 'Be careful. Text if you find anything.'

It took us less than five minutes to find a likely looking spot, next to a sign bearing the name of the road. While I texted Celestine, Jeremy spread the tartan blanket he'd produced from the boot of his car across the fierce-looking spikes and reached into his pocket.

'Flip you for it,' he said, flashing a silver coin at me. 'Heads or tails?'

I shook my bedraggled hair out of my eyes and peered at the fence apprehensively; it was all right for him, he wasn't vertically challenged. 'Maybe we should wait for the others,' I said, chewing my lip. 'Celestine knows first aid.'

Jeremy smiled wryly. 'I know. She saved my life, remember?'

It was how they'd met; Jeremy had been stabbed and Celestine had found him. But my faith in my aunt's medical skills wasn't enough to inspire me to scale a two metre spiked fence. 'Or I could find another way in.'

He raised an eyebrow. 'Come on, Skye, this isn't like you. Where's that ballsy attitude I've seen so often?'

I gazed at the fence; had it grown in the last minute? Then I thought of Nico and Owen, and what would happen to both of them if we didn't reach the cottage in time. Clenching my teeth, I planted a soggy trainer on the sign and pulled myself up. With difficulty, I hoisted one leg over the blanket and teetered. 'Now what?'

Clasping his hands together, he hooked them under my foot on his side of the fence. 'Swing your other leg over. I'll take your weight.'

With a confidence I didn't feel, I did as I was told. For one second, I hung in the air, suspended by Jeremy's fingers around my foot. Then a sudden gust of wind hit me and with all the elegance of a pregnant hippo, I toppled sideways. Jeremy clambered hurriedly over as I got to my feet, brushing dirt and leaves off my clothes and hair. Unfortunately he didn't stick the landing either.

'Ow!' he howled from the undergrowth. 'Bloody stinging nettles.'

I stuck out a hand to help him. 'Are you OK?'

Smoothing his hair, he nodded. 'Let's pretend that didn't happen.'

'Glad to see you two negotiated the fence safely,' my aunt called, peering through the iron poles. She clambered gracefully over, making me feel even more hippo-esque. Once Gregor was inside, we cut through the trees in watchful silence and headed towards the cottage, branches and leaves rustling overhead as the wind whipped through them.

Mary materialised on the path, looming in front of us like a banshee tracker scout. 'It is as thy lover said. They weave their dark arts in the keeper's house over yonder.'

Up until then, I'd subconsciously been hoping Owen had got cold feet and backed out. Mary's comment told me he hadn't. Gregor looked at Celestine. 'You have the tools for the job?'

She patted her pocket. 'Yes.'

'Then there is no time to lose. If we succeed, the Solomonarii will be angry. We should be ready to flee at haste.'

I shivered and tried not to think about what would happen if Nico's father suspected his son of tipping us off. He'd beaten him for snooping in his study – what punishment would he dish out for an outright betrayal? We'd just have to hope he never found out the truth.

Once the cottage loomed into sight, my stomach began to gurgle with tension. It was hard to see in the darkness but it looked like the windows were missing and half the roof had fallen in. Faint lights flickered through the gaps in the walls; torches, I guessed, or maybe candles. I had no idea what we'd find inside but my brain seemed to be re-running every horror film I'd ever subjected it to. Ivan Albescu was a cross between Dracula and Dr Frankenstein and Owen had turned into one of the creatures from *Zombieland*. I shook the images away and huddled inside my coat, trying to ignore the biting wind.

'At least the rain is stopping,' Jeremy whispered as we approached the cottage.

I lifted my chin, then held out a hand; he was right, the needle-sharp sting of the rain had stopped. 'There's no wind, either.'

Gregor lowered his hood. 'They have the power to control the weather,' he reminded us. 'Wind and rain do not make it easy to keep a lighted flame.'

I glanced at my watch; it was ten to midnight. 'What if they've started already?'

Gregor shook his head. 'They will not begin until the witching hour. It strengthens the ritual.'

I was still clinging to the idea that we could stop the spell before they began. 'What are we waiting for? Let's go!'

Reaching into her pockets, Celestine pulled out cling-film twists and handed them to each of us, except for Mary. 'Salt and black pepper, just in case one of us misses.'

As much as I trusted Gregor's advice, I still couldn't imagine how seasoning could be so powerful. But it wasn't the time to raise it; I had to hope he really did know what he was doing.

'They are but three, in the foremost room,' Mary said, pointing towards the dim glow I'd noticed. 'I dared not go nearer for fear they sensed my presence and two spirits became Eaten this night.'

I fired a sharp look her way. 'No spirits are getting Eaten tonight, OK?'

She returned my glare but said nothing. Celestine looked between the two of us. 'Stop it, you two. We've got enough enemies here without squabbling amongst ourselves.'

She was right, of course. 'Sorry,' I mumbled and Mary did the same.

'The ritual will be stronger if the power of three is called upon. We will enter through the back of the house.' Gregor checked the time and signalled us to move forward. 'Stay low and follow me. Jeremy, you bring up the rear. If we get separated, meet at the Lodge Gate.'

And then we were creeping forwards in the eerie stillness, edging nearer to the house. Mary hung back, her face a mirror of the anxiety I felt. As we got closer, I could hear a low chanting but couldn't make out any words.

'Romanian, an old cleansing spell,' Gregor whispered. 'And so it begins.'

Fear mingled with adrenaline spiked its way through my veins. My fingers gripped the small twist of salt as though my life depended on it. I forced them to relax; if I wasn't careful I'd tear the delicate plastic and the only thing I'd be covering would be my pocket.

'You OK, Skye?' Jeremy said, his voice barely carrying through the night air.

I nodded at the same moment as we reached the back of the cottage. Gregor turned and placed a finger to his lips. Holding up a hand, he pointed to Jeremy and me and indicated we should head towards the window. Then he touched Celestine and himself and pointed inside. My aunt reached out to grasp my hand hard. I returned the squeeze. Then she was gone. I drew in a shallow breath and followed Jeremy to the glassless window.

For a full minute, neither of us dared to poke our heads over the windowsill. Crouched low underneath the rotting, ivy-covered ledge, we listened to the rise and fall of the chant. Then Jeremy waved his thumb at me. I tipped my head in agreement and we peered into the room.

I spotted Nico first. He was standing furthest away from me, in a corner of the small room. Lanterns hung here and there from the wooden ceiling beams, casting strange shadows against the crumbling walls. Even in the half-light, his bruises stood out. His expression was pinched and anxious and I decided he looked pretty much like I felt. Every now and then, he glanced uneasily around and I guessed he must be wondering if I was coming.

Owen was in the middle of the room, inside a circle of what appeared to be black rope. Any last hope I'd been nurturing about somehow preventing the ritual from even starting evaporated. Gregor had been crystal clear: to interfere with the spell at the wrong time would be catastrophic. It looked like Owen's salvation really did lie with simple seasoning.

He was the complete opposite of Nico, a look of relaxed anticipation written across his features and I remembered how he enjoyed risky situations. As Gregor had predicted, there was a chalk pentagram inside the rope and Owen stood at the very centre. A tall black candle burned at each of the five points of the symbol. The flames hardly flickered and once again I marvelled at the difference in the weather here and how it had been two hundred metres away, where the wind would have extinguished the candles in an instant. Was Nico holding the rain at bay or was it his father? Either way, it was an impressive feat.

On the outside of the circle, with their backs to the internal doorway, were two men. One was tall and dark; I recognised him as Nico's dad. The other was shorter and muscular, with glistening, slicked-back hair and a raven-black beard; I'd never seen him before. He held a square stone, which I assumed was one of the talismans Gregor had told us about. Ivan was reading from it.

Beside them was a low table, with a dark chalice on it and a flaming blood-red candle.

Ducking down again, I tugged back the sleeve of my coat; eleven fifty-eight. In two more minutes, the ritual would begin. I rubbed a finger over the salt packet and hoped I'd know when to use it if I had to. Gregor had said we'd know when to throw it – what if we didn't and missed the crucial point?

Not for the first time, I wished Celestine was next to me. I suspected Gregor had sent me around the outside so that I could run more easily if I needed to, but I wanted the reassurance of my aunt and, as lovely as he could be, Jeremy wasn't quite the same.

The chanting stopped. The air hung in expectant silence. I raised my head slowly and peered into the room.

Ivan was standing opposite Owen, his feet a short distance from the dirt circle. 'It is time,' Ivan said, his unaccented voice carrying across the unnatural quiet. 'Are you ready?'

Owen smiled and I saw his mouth twist in a way that was familiar and strange to me at the same time. When this was over we had a lot of talking to do. 'Of course,' he said, with a confidence I wasn't sure he really felt. 'Bring it on.'

Ivan nodded. 'Nico, seal the room so that no one can disturb our work.'

Nico went to the corner of the room and lifted a black bag. Carefully, he tilted it and a thin stream of dark powder flowed onto the ground. Leaving a continuous line of the substance behind him, he edged around the outside of the room. When he reached the gap in the wall where the front door once was, he paused and looked out. Anxiously, I craned my head around but all I saw was trees. What would Nico do if he spotted Mary hovering on the tree-line? I hadn't told him I was bringing a ghost of my own. Would he realise Mary was there to help? But I needn't have worried – she must have moved out of sight. Nico tilted the bag once more and continued with his task.

Jeremy and I flattened ourselves against the cold ground as he approached the window and I resisted the temptation to let Nico know we were there; I didn't know how he'd react and wanted to avoid making his father suspicious. Leaves tickled my face and the smell of damp earth filled my nostrils. Heart galloping, I tried not to think about how many creepy crawlies I was getting up close and personal with; now was not the time to break out in arachnophobia.

When Nico neared the door at the back of the room, the breath froze in my lungs. Gregor and Celestine must be well inside the house by now. If Nico saw them, I hoped he'd know they were on his side. He paused in the doorway and stared into the blackness beyond. Seconds stretched. Then Nico lowered the bag of powder and began to pour again. I allowed myself a silent sigh of relief when he bowed to his father. 'Done.'

As Nico crossed the room and took up his position at the foot of the pentagram, I saw his gaze flicker towards the window. I wished there was some way to reassure him that he wasn't alone, but it was impossible without giving everything away to his father and the other man. I wasn't sure I wanted Owen to know we were there, either. Somehow, I doubted he'd appreciate my interference.

Ivan gestured to the bearded man, who took the red candle from the table and carried it to the edge of the room. He touched it to the powder and a brilliant blue flash seared into my retinas as the flame chased around the room. It burned for a few seconds and then went out. The smell of putrid eggs filled the air and I tried not to gag as I twisted away from the window to gulp in mouthfuls of fresh air. Blinking furiously to clear the after-image, I tried to remember where I'd smelled such a stench before.

'Sulphur,' Jeremy breathed. 'But what does it do?'

I didn't have the faintest idea but I guessed it must have magical properties. All I knew was that the smell made me feel sick to my stomach.

'We should begin,' the man said, dragging my attention back to the cottage. I was surprised to hear a thick Scottish accent colouring his words. Glaswegian, I thought. 'The seal will only last an hour.'

Ivan nodded. The other man handed him the talisman

and reached towards the table to collect the chalice. Making his way around the edge of the circle, he handed the candle to Nico, who took it without speaking. Once past him, the man stopped, facing the window directly opposite us. On instinct, I ducked, wincing at the shooting pains the movement sent through my groaning thigh muscles. It was a few seconds before I realised that the foliage climbing up the walls hid us from sight and I dared to straighten up and look into the room again.

Ivan held up the talisman and began to speak once more. The words meant nothing to me and I guessed he must be speaking Romanian again. Then he switched into English.

'Dust of the grave, we invoke thee,' he called, and cast a handful of black grit across the pentagram. Owen flinched as the particles passed through him. Stomach churning with tension, I studied him. So far he looked exactly the same as always and I wondered at what point in the ritual we'd see the first signs of change.

The shorter man reached into his jacket and withdrew a steel knife. Lifting the goblet, he dipped the shining blade into it and flicked it into the circle. 'Water of the dead, we implore thee.'

Several seconds ticked by and I saw Nico's gaze slide hesitantly towards the door to the back room. Then he cleared his throat and said in a faltering tone, 'Candle of the eternal night, we command thee.'

I craned sideways to see if I could catch a glimpse of Gregor or Celestine but the doorway was dark. Jeremy nudged me; the candles inside the pentagram were starting to flicker. A puzzled frown creased my forehead; there was no breeze that I could feel but Nico had said that controlling the weather took concentration. Maybe the ritual was making it hard to keep the wind and rain at bay?

Owen was still looking calm and relaxed in the centre of the pentagram. Ivan reached down to the table and lifted a length of black cloth. Slowly, he peeled back the material. The candlelight flashed as it caught a slender copper blade as long as my forearm. Slowly, Ivan raised it up until it was head height. He smiled and all three of the Solomonarii opened their mouths to speak in unison.

'Tempest of the damned, we summon thee.'

A sudden howling sprang up and the flames of the candles flattened for a moment before righting themselves. Air whirled around my face but the rest of my body felt nothing, as though the wind was only blowing inside the cottage. I held out a hand in the night air to confirm my suspicions: there was no wind outside. Jeremy looked at me, his expression equally confused.

Inside, Ivan was chanting again but it was harder to hear him over the roaring of the wind. I caught snatches of words but couldn't make out any meaning. Then he tilted the knife towards Owen's forehead. It hovered there for a nanosecond, then descended and made contact. My breath caught in my throat. Behind Owen's head, where he couldn't possibly see it, a yawning black chasm had opened. Ivan spoke again and the blade travelled down to touch Owen's chest. The void increased. Here and there, I caught a faint flicker of red, like a scarlet tongue licking at the darkness. Owen was blissfully unaware of what was happening behind him. My teeth gnawed at my lip; every nerve in my body wanted to scream that something was wrong. But Owen simply smiled.

My eyes flew to Nico. All colour had drained from his face. Even his bruises appeared bloodless and he looked ill. Beside me, Jeremy's expression was equally strained. My fingers brushed the cling-film in my pocket and I pulled it out in readiness. He nodded once and held up his own twist of speckled pepper. In the back room, I pictured Celestine and Gregor doing the same.

'Not yet,' Jeremy whispered, jerking his head towards the room again.

Now Ivan was drawing the knife past Owen's waist towards the floor and the chasm was almost as tall as he was. More than one sliver of crimson writhed within its inky depths now. After kneeling at Owen's feet for a few seconds, Ivan rose and stood before the ghost, his lips moving feverishly. The roar of the wind increased, I had no idea how the candles were still alight. Then, in one fluid movement, he raised the blade high and, clasping it with two hands, plunged it deep into Owen's chest.

I couldn't help it; I let out a silent scream. Owen's eyes widened in shock and his mouth sagged. The black chasm oozed forwards to envelop him and I saw his hands clawing against it as it wrapped itself around his face. Again, a soundless scream escaped me.

'Help me!' Owen shrieked but none of the Solomonarii moved. Ivan and the other man looked on impassively but Nico was rooted to the spot, an expression of sick horror crawling across his features. I jumped to my feet and his eyes met mine, flooded with incomprehension. Then my gaze was dragged back to Owen, struggling to free himself. Tugging at the plastic in my hand, I flung it into the room. There was a sizzling sound and a flash of blue fire. I turned back to see Jeremy staring in shock at the window.

'It evaporated,' he said, pushing his fingers towards the gap. Blue sparks flew and he snatched his hand back. 'Like there was a forcefield in the way.'

To my right, I registered two flashes of blue in the doorway to the back room and I guessed Celestine and Gregor had thrown their salt and pepper as well. Jeremy drew back his hand to throw his and I pulled it down. 'Don't. That's what Nico was doing – sealing the room. I guess that means we can't get in.'

Tears welled in my eyes and Owen's struggles grew weaker and he sank to his knees. Helplessly, I watched as Ivan closed his eyes and continued his frantic chanting.

The other man joined in. The darkness covered Owen completely. For a moment, he was a black silhouette in the candlelight. Then the black melted away, leaving him huddled on his knees. He raised his head and looked around, as though seeing for the first time. Sobbing, I peered at him; he looked no different, maybe Gregor had been wrong. Then he turned his head towards the window and I saw his eyes. Where once they'd been the grey of stormy skies, now they were oily depths of blackness. Climbing to his feet, he bared his teeth in a wolfish grin. Ivan gestured at him and Owen parted his lips to howl. Inside the scarlet gash of the opening was a blood-red forked tongue.

My own mouth fell open in horror. Whatever it was in there, it wasn't Owen and I had no idea if the real Owen was still inside, fighting to get out. Desperately, I looked at Nico. He slowly edged round the circle to me. 'Help him!' I hissed, snatching the cling-film from Jeremy. 'Throw this at the pentagram!'

For a second, I thought he would ignore me. Then he strode across the room and reached through the window, blue light parting around the hand that had cast the sealing spell. I thrust the twist into Nico's hand. 'Quickly!'

His fingers pressed hard into mine. Then, eyes fixed on his oblivious father, Nico opened the plastic and hurled the contents high over the pentagram. Salt and pepper danced in the wind and, seemingly in slow motion, settled over the thing which used to be Owen. It screamed as though burned and fell back to its knees. Ivan stopped his chanting and stared. Bubbling blisters appeared on the creature's cheeks and black blood erupted in jagged spurts. It screamed again and I noticed that a yawning white hole had appeared in the floor. As I watched in terror, the Owen-thing began to slide into it, as though dragged by an invisible weight. It scrabbled at the floor as the blackness seeped out of it. I stared, searching for a sign that Owen was still there and thought I caught a flash of gold in the dark eyes. Then the wind reached hurricane force and with one gust the candles went out. A sudden boom filled the air and the room was filled with brilliant white light. When it faded, the room was utterly silent and the Solomonarii were crumpled heaps on the floor. There was no sign of Owen at all.

'Nico,' I yelled and stumbled to my feet.

I took a few steps towards the door before Jeremy pulled me back. 'He's still breathing. Come on, we have to go.'

My eyes were dragged back to the spot where Owen had been. 'We can't leave. What about Nico? And I need to find Owen.'

Celestine and Gregory raced around the side of the house. 'Owen is gone,' she said, her tone broken. 'And from what I saw, we're lucky he is.'

I rounded on her. 'How can you say that?'

She grasped my arms. 'That wasn't him at the end. And wherever he is now, he wouldn't have wanted to be the creature they made him.'

The shock caught up with me and I felt my face crumple. 'But where is he?'

Her expression softened. 'I don't know. If it helps, white light is usually a good sign.'

I stared at her, willing her to be right. 'He's really gone?'

She nodded.

Fresh tears coursed down my face. 'But I didn't get to say goodbye. I didn't get to tell him anything.'

Celestine pulled me close and let me sob a moment. 'I know. But if it's any consolation, I think he realised there are things worse than death right there at the end. You and Nico saved him from that at least.'

My eyes strayed back to the window. 'Nico. I need to see him.'

Gregor cast a grim glance over his shoulder. 'We should not linger here. When the Solomonarii awake, they will be angry.'

A stab of anxiety cut into me. 'Nico's father will kill him.'

Gregor looked solemn. 'Events happened very quickly. If Nico is lucky, the others will remember little of the details tonight and assume the ritual went wrong of its own accord.'

'No, we can't take the chance.' I pushed my aunt away.

'Nico risked everything to save Owen. I won't abandon him.'

For a moment, I thought Jeremy would argue. Then he turned and dashed towards the cottage. Before Celestine could stop me, I followed.

Nico stayed motionless as we ran into the room. His purple bruises were indistinguishable from the thick black dust which covered his face. Jeremy gave his shoulder an urgent shake. 'Nico, wake up!'

Precious seconds ticked by as I willed Nico to open his eyes. 'Please wake up,' I begged, my gaze flickering to the slumped bodies of the other Solomonarii. 'We don't have much time.'

Silence hung in the air. Then Nico let out a weak cough and his eyes twitched open. 'Skye?' he croaked.

'I'm here,' I murmured. 'But we have to get out of here now.'

'Any broken bones?' Jeremy asked.

Nico coughed again. 'No, but my head feels like the roof fell on it.'

Jeremy pulled him to his feet. 'I've got a few paracetamol in the car. Let's go and get them.'

In other circumstances, I might have been amused at his practicality but I felt like my mouth would never smile again.

Nico glanced at the prone body of his father and hesitated. 'Is he . . . ?'

I shook my head. 'Still breathing. But there's no way you can stay with him now. He'll know something went wrong. He'll never trust you again and think what he'd do to you.'

Pressing his lips together, Nico bowed his head. 'I know.'

I reached out and took his hand. 'Come with me. We'll help you.'

He nodded wordlessly and we began to make our way outside. Then he stopped. 'Wait!'

Lurching forwards, he bent to pluck the square talisman his father had been using from the ground. He waved it at me, a grim expression on his face. 'If they come for me, I want to be ready.'

A low groan sounded from the bearded man and Jeremy jerked his hand towards the door. 'Hurry!'

We didn't need to be told twice. Hand in hand, Nico and I followed him to join the others. As we melted into the trees, I remembered the look on Owen's face as he'd disappeared and I bit back a sob. More than anything, I wanted him to appear beside me, grinning about another close shave but I knew that was never going to happen. He was gone and no amount of wishing would ever bring him back.

Chapter 19

The journey back to the car was a blur. None of us had much to say and even Mary, who hadn't seen exactly what had happened, seemed to know better than to ask questions. By the time we'd said a grave goodbye to Gregor, my numbed emotions were starting to thaw out and the pain began to seep in. Even nestling into Nico's shoulder and feeling his arm around me didn't help.

I didn't speak as Jeremy guided his Nissan Micra along the sleep-stilled roads. In halting words, Celestine put Mary out of her misery, although she'd guessed some of what had happened from the conversation outside the cottage. Mary listened in uncharacteristic silence. It wasn't until my aunt had told the whole horrific tale that questions started to throng in my mind.

'We exorcised him, didn't we?' I asked in a dull

monotone. 'We sent him somewhere terrible.'

There was a brief moment of quiet, then Celestine answered. 'In a way. Like I said before, when there's a white light at the end, it usually means the ghost is passing across. The transition is less peaceful than we're used to but I think they end up in the same place.'

'But you don't actually know for sure,' I said and a note of bitterness crept into my voice. 'All that crap about saving him and we've got no idea what happened.'

My aunt studied me. 'We did the best we could,' she said softly. 'Owen made some bad choices. We should be glad we were able to do anything at all. If it hadn't been for Nico here, I dread to think what might have happened.'

Nico looked pensive. 'The Solomonarii did this to him. I feel bad about that.'

Jeremy watched him in the rear-view mirror. 'Without you, he might have suffered a much worse fate.'

His words reminded me that Nico had lost plenty, too. 'What are you going to do?' I asked. 'There's no way you can go back home.'

He ran a shaky hand over his face. 'I don't know. I think my mum's sister might still live in London but I don't know where.'

Celestine turned in her seat. 'We'll help you find her. And in the meantime, you're welcome to stay with us.'

Nico smiled. 'Thanks,' he said, sounding grateful. 'I'd like that.'

Now that I knew Nico had somewhere to go, the ache of Owen's loss took over again. 'Isn't there any way we can try to contact ghosts who've passed across, to see if any of them know anything about Owen?'

Mary bared her teeth in a stumpy growl. 'There are those who would say aye but that path is shrouded in darkness. Naught but the foolhardiest of men chooseth to walk it.'

Celestine's face crinkled in sympathy. 'I know it hurts but, wherever he is, he's better off there than staying here as one of the Eaten.'

I gazed at her for several long seconds before turning my head to stare at the blacked-out streets, unable to shake the feeling that we hadn't saved Owen at all. Closing my eyes, I leaned my forehead against the cold window and tried to block out the image of him scrambling on the ground, trying to find a handhold on the dusty cottage floor. In my mind, I saw the flash of amber in his eyes in the last seconds before he'd disappeared and I knew I'd be seeing it in my dreams for a long time. Nico squeezed my shoulder in wordless sympathy and wiped away the single tear trickling down my cheek. For the first time since I'd understood what being psychic really meant, I'd failed to help a ghost find peace. It was something I'd have to live with until the day I died. If I was really unlucky, it wouldn't end there.

Chapter 20

Hyde Park was busy again. I wasn't surprised. It was the weekend and the weather was glorious; any Londoners who hadn't escaped the city were making the most of the sunshine all across the city's open spaces and Hyde Park was no exception.

I was sitting by the Serpentine, waiting for Cerys, the way I had every weekend for the five weeks since Owen disappeared. The water glittered as the sunlight danced across it but I couldn't bring myself to look for long. It reminded me of Owen and the thought of him still made me ache inside. I didn't think the guilt would ever go, no matter how often Celestine and Jeremy told me not to blame myself, that I couldn't have foreseen the terrible events of that night in the woods. In my mind, I could still see that inky blackness consuming him and feel his fear as the full horror hit him.

'Hello again,' Cerys said, stopping on the path in front of me and smiling. 'You're here more often than I am these days.'

I swallowed and returned her smile. 'It looks that way, doesn't it? How are you?'

She sat beside me and proceeded to fill me in on everything that had happened in the week since I'd last seen her. She was coping with revision for her end of year exams, she said, and looking forward to a week off school at half-term. Her parents had agreed to let her stay overnight at a friend's house in a few weeks, which they'd refused to consider in the months immediately after her brother's death. In fact, she said, they seemed to be OK. Not great, but getting better.

I listened, wondering whether this would be the week I'd tell her the truth about how I'd met Owen. After he'd gone, I'd been restless and found my troubled spirit soothed at the lake. The first time I'd met her had been an accident – she'd been there, staring at the water and we'd exchanged half-smiles. Then I'd remembered that I'd wanted Owen to talk to her through me and I'd hung around the following week, hoping to bump into her. Now I looked forward to our chats; I liked hearing about Owen's family and I was glad they were healing the wound his death had left in their lives. It made me feel a little less desolate.

'Mum started talking about going back to work this week,' Cerys said, leaning back in the seat and stretching in a way that reminded me of her brother all over again. 'Only part-time but it's better than nothing.'

I smiled. 'That's great, Cerys. I bet Owen would be pleased, too.'

'Yeah, I think he would.' Her expression grew thoughtful. 'You're going to think this is weird but I used to talk to him all the time here. It felt like he could hear me, even if he never answered, like when he had his iPod on and was pretending not to listen.'

I swallowed. 'That doesn't sound weird.'

Cerys sighed. 'I told him all kinds of stuff, things I'd never have said when he was alive.' She grimaced. 'I think I even told him I loved him, which I definitely never said to his face.'

I blinked and looked away before she saw my eyes swimming with tears. 'Some people think the dead still hear us.'

Nodding, she said, 'Yeah, I know. But lately, it feels different here, like he's not – I don't know – listening any more. I miss him.' Shaking her head, she gave an embarrassed little laugh. 'You probably think I'm mental.'

I squeezed my eyes closed. 'No.'

Cerys leaned towards me, her grey eyes filled with concern. 'Have I upset you or something?'

Opening my eyes, I gazed at her. 'Suppose I told you

that you were right all those times you thought Owen was nearby, listening to you?'

She grinned. 'Now who'd be being mental? There's no such thing as ghosts.'

'That's pretty much what he said, the first time I met him,' I replied. 'Even though he was one.'

There was a long silence. Cerys stared at me and the grin slid from her face. 'You're being serious.'

I nodded. 'You know I never mentioned exactly where I knew him from? That's because I didn't meet him until after he'd drowned.'

Her mouth fell open. 'You actually expect me to believe you see dead people? Like on that film?'

She could have meant any one of a number of films; I didn't ask which one. 'All the time.'

'Shut up,' she said, her tone a mixture of scorn and curiosity. 'You're making it up.'

I chose my next words with care. Whatever I said could tip the balance one way or another. 'When you were younger, Owen told me you used to love the Teletubbies.'

She frowned. 'So did every other kid my age. It doesn't mean my dead brother told you about it.'

I dredged my memory for other things Owen had told me. 'You wet the bed when you went to stay with your grandparents and told them it was him. It was your pogo stick he borrowed when he cut his face. You used to have a teddy bear called Jock and you wouldn't let anyone touch it apart from you and Owen.' My heart thudding against my ribs, I met her incredulous gaze. 'His greatest dream was to drive at Silverstone, although he'd have settled for Brand's Hatch, and he was the South-East England go-karting champion when he was ten.'

A look of pure confusion crossed her face. 'How do you know all this stuff?'

Projecting a calmness I didn't feel, I smiled. 'Owen told me. About a month ago.'

She shifted on the bench and, for a minute, I thought she'd bolt and I'd never see her again. I watched as she struggled to absorb what I'd told her. 'I don't believe in the afterlife.'

'It exists. Some people die and pass across to the astral plane straight away. Others, like Owen, stay for a while.' I hesitated, unwilling to reveal what had really happened to her brother. 'There are ghosts everywhere.'

Her gaze slid sideways. 'Is – is he here now?'

I swallowed and drew in a deep breath. 'No. He moved on a few weeks ago.'

She folded her arms. 'Good, because I'd take back all that soppy stuff if he was.'

I clenched my hands into fists. 'You believe me, then?'

'I dunno. Maybe.' Eyes wide, she stared at me. 'Just saying I do believe you, if he's not here, where is he? Heaven?'

I'd been expecting this question and had rehearsed my answer over and over. But as easy as it would have been to agree with her, I couldn't. 'I don't know. No one does, for certain.'

Cerys sank into the bench and tilted her head back to stare at the sky. 'My parents used to worry about me coming here all the time.' She let out a shaky laugh. 'They had no idea I'd meet someone like you.'

I wasn't sure what she meant by that but it didn't sound entirely complimentary. She wasn't convinced, I realised, which made me wish even more that I'd spoken to her while Owen was still around so that he could help prove that he was really there. A familiar dull ache started in my chest as I once again wished things had ended differently. 'He used to tell me he'd let you down. Did he?'

She looked searchingly into my eyes before shaking her head. 'No. I suppose I did blame him at first, especially when my parents were struggling to cope. But I never could stay angry with him for long, not even when he was doing his smug older brother thing. One flash of that cheeky grin and I'd forgive him.'

I knew exactly what she meant. The memory of it cut at my heart. 'He had it tough, too. I think he regretted a lot of things but more than anything, he was sorry for the pain he caused you.'

Lapsing into silence, I stared at the island on the lake.

It was harder than I'd expected, talking about Owen with her. She was handling it much better than I was.

'Skye?' Cerys broke into my thoughts and laid her hand on my arm. 'I don't know if what you're telling me is true but, if it is, then I'm glad he wasn't alone. It must have been hard for him, watching us moping around. Thank you.'

I couldn't help it; a sob escaped me. Pressing my lips together, I struggled to get my emotions under control. 'You're welcome. I liked him a lot.'

Cerys gazed at me, her shimmering grey eyes so similar to her brother's that it hurt. 'I can see that,' she said, and a wobbly smile crossed her face. 'Look at the pair of us, snivelling away. Wherever he is, I bet he's making girls cry there as well.'

Once again, the image of Owen kneeling on the floor of the cottage flashed into my mind. Firmly, I pushed it away and attempted a smile of my own. 'You're probably right.'

'I saw your Friend Request on Owen's page, by the way,' she said. 'I look after it now. You don't mind if I don't accept it?'

I'd forgotten all about that; it seemed like a lifetime ago now. But I could hardly blame her for knocking me back. Besides, what reason could I have for wanting it now, anyway? 'No, I don't mind.'

She looked relieved. 'Only, I think we'll close his page.

Eventually, people will stop coming to it and it will make it feel like they're forgetting him. I don't want that.' Then she threw me a sideways glance. 'You could always add me, if you wanted to?'

'You know, I might do that,' I replied. 'I bet you've got plenty of stories to share about Owen.'

Cerys grinned, a wicked look in her eyes. 'Trust me, I do. Did he ever mention his obsession with the Go Go Bunnies?'

Nico waited until I'd waved goodbye to Cerys before he joined me on the bench.

'Well?' he asked. 'Did you tell her?'

Nodding, I watched Cerys as she disappeared behind the trees. 'Yeah. She took it pretty well, all things considered.'

'You mean she didn't call you a nut-job or run away screaming,' Nico replied, looping an arm around my shoulders. 'Sensible girl. How are you doing?'

I thought about that. Since the night at the cottage we'd been closer than ever; we'd all slept in the next day but Nico and I spent hours talking things through once we'd woken up. Recognising we had a lot to sort out, Celestine and Jeremy had given us some space and, even though Nico and I were shocked to our core by what we'd been through, the time we spent together reminded me of everything I loved about him. Once he'd moved out to live with the family Celestine and Jeremy had tracked down for him, I had to settle for long phone calls and snatched meetings. We were trying to take things slowly, though. A lot had changed since the last time we'd been together. I needed to come to terms with what had happened to Owen and the colossal guilt it had given me. For his part, Nico was busy settling into his new life and was learning all kinds of things about his parents' true relationship. It seemed much of what Nico had been told by his father was untrue and only added to our conviction that Nico had got out in the nick of time. There was no sign that Ivan Albescu was searching for his son but none of us doubted it was only a matter of time before the Solomonarii began to hunt him down. Nico had already begun to prepare for the showdown. He'd stayed in touch with Gregor and was learning all he could about the Solomonarii to prepare himself. He wanted to be ready when they came.

In the meantime, he was enjoying getting to know his new family and it made me glad to see him more settled. The downside was that he was further away and attending another school. We'd reluctantly agreed to limit our contact as much as we could in case Ivan was watching me, but I already missed seeing Nico every day at school.

'I'm OK,' I answered, with a weak smile. 'Not great but I'm getting there.'

Returning my smile, he ruffled my hair. 'You'd better be going. You wouldn't want to miss the wedding of the year.'

I grinned. I didn't know about wedding of the year, but Isobel and Pete's marriage could certainly lay claim to being the weirdest I'd ever been invited to; after all, it wasn't every day I got to be bridesmaid to a ghost. At least the bride wouldn't be swamped in a meringue of ivory taffeta and the best man wouldn't try to get off with me. Or I hoped he wouldn't; the thought of Gawjus George swooping in for a slobbery snog made me feel ill.

Checking my watch, I nodded. 'I suppose so.'

His dark eyes glittered. 'I'd like to go to this Dearly D place one day. I've heard plenty about it.'

'You'd be welcome, once the Solomonarii have given up looking for you.'

We stared into each other's eyes, both knowing it was time for goodbye again but neither of us wanting to say it.

'I'll see you on Facebook, then?' Nico said eventually.

I blinked, willing my tears to subside; crying came too easily to me these days. 'Yeah.'

He gazed solemnly down at me and placed a lingering kiss on my lips. 'I love you, Skye Thackery. Never forget that, no matter what happens.'

My heart swelled with bitter-sweet happiness. It was hard to believe that I'd almost hated him a few months ago; now I could hardly bear for us to be apart. Wrapping my arms around him, I absorbed the hug, inhaling a lungful of his scent to carry with me after he'd gone. 'I love you, too,' I murmured.

Nico leaned down and kissed me again. The touch of his lips caused an explosion of electricity to run down my spine. Closing my eyes, I drank in the sweetness of his mouth against mine. This was what kissing was meant to feel like, not the feather-like brush of lips that weren't really there and the realisation tugged at my emotions. Even if Owen had been alive, he could never have competed with Nico.

Unwillingly, we broke apart.

'Be careful,' I said, my voice breaking on the words.

He raised his hand to touch my cheek, then backed away. 'Always.'

Feeling as though my heart would break, I watched him until he was out of sight then psyched myself up for the long trek home. As I headed towards Marble Arch tube station, I knew two things: one, I was deeply in love with Nico and two, I had to let him go, for now at least. It was too risky to see each other while his father was searching for him. I could only hope our separation wouldn't last long because, if Owen Wicks had taught me anything, it was to live each day as though it was my last. And I wanted to spend as many of them as I could with Nico.

Acknowledgements

Sometimes, writers make up more than just their characters and plots. I'm no exception, so I should probably point out that the boats on the Serpentine are specifically designed not to tip over, in case anyone was planning a re-enactment. Also, there is no deserted cottage in Highgate Woods, so if you're looking to do a little black magic, you'll have to find somewhere else to go.

As always, my biggest thanks go to Lee, for keeping me supplied with Jelly Tots, and Tania, for not eating all of them. Love ya.

Massive hugs are also due to:

Richard and Janice, for being my cheerleaders.

Clare, for nagging and nagging to read the early draft – I might still be writing it if you hadn't.

Jo Williamson at Antony Harwood Ltd, for her unceasing patience and lovely lunches. Here's to the next year!

Brenda, Ruth, Melissa, Vivien, Elaine and the whole team at Piccadilly Press, for pulling out all the stops. Thank you – I really appreciate your vision and hard work.

Sharon Birch and Esther Shawe for their invaluable advice on everything to do with falling through ice and near-drowning – you were both brilliant!

My fellow Sisterbloggers; Keren David, Sophia Bennett, Luisa Plaja, Cat Clarke, Gillian Philip, Kay Woodward, Keris Stainton and Fiona Dunbar – you give great support, ladies.

And lastly, thanks to you, the reader, who brings the story to life. I'll keep writing as long as you're there :)

Discover what happened with Lucy and Jeremy . . .

My So-Called Afterlife

TAMSYN MURRAY

'Aaargh!' Stumbling backwards, the man's face flooded with horrified embarrassment. 'How long have you been standing there?'
My mind fizzed furiously. He could see me. He could actually see me! I could have hugged him! Well, I couldn't, but you know what I mean.

Fifteen-year-old Lucy has been stuck in the men's loos since she was murdered there six months ago and Jeremy is the first person who's been able to see or hear her. Just her luck that he's a seriously uncool geography-teacher type – but at least he's determined to help.

Once he's found a way for her to leave the loos, she's soon meeting other ghosts, including the gorgeous Ryan. However, when Jeremy insists that she helps him track down her killer, she has to confront her greatest fear . . .

Spirits, spells and bad boy hell . . .

My So-Called Haunting

TAMSYN MURRAY

Skye, a fourteen-year-old who can see ghosts,
is very stressed. Not only is the ghost of a
sixteenth-century witch giving her fashion tips,
but she's struggling to settle into life with her aunt,
and is developing a crush on the most
unattainable boy in the school, Nico.

When her aunt asks for her help with a troubled
teen ghost called Dontay, she's glad of the distraction.
But then Nico starts paying her attention,
and she's soon facing a battle to keep her
love life and her psychic life separate.

As things get ever more complicated, it looks as
though Dontay's past might cost Skye her future.